"You have a lot of unpaid bills," Jack said softly.

"And you have a lot of nerve." Ondine's eyes narrowed on his face. After yanking open the drawer, she stuffed the envelopes inside, then slammed it shut.

"Putting them in there's not going to help make them go away."

"Well luckily for you, how I make them go away is none of your business," she snapped.

Jack was leaning against the counter, sunlight and shadow crossing his face. "But it could be," he said after a moment.

She glared at him.

"What would you say if I told you that I could make all of those bills just disappear?"

"I would say that you probably need to go back to the hospital for a CT scan on your head," she said stiffly.

He smiled then, a quick, devastating smile that made her breath catch. "And on any other day I'd probably agree with you, but today is different. I have a proposition, a proposal really. And if you provide the service, I would be willing to generously recompense you."

"What's the proposition?" she asked. The room was starting to spin.

"I want you to marry me."

Louise Fuller was a tomboy who hated pink and always wanted to be the prince—not the princess! Now she enjoys creating heroines who aren't pretty pushovers but are strong, believable women. Before writing for Harlequin, she studied literature and philosophy at university, then worked as a reporter on her local newspaper. She lives in Royal Tunbridge Wells with her impossibly handsome husband, Patrick, and their six children.

Books by Louise Fuller

Harlequin Presents

The Man She Should Have Married
Italian's Scandalous Marriage Plan
Beauty in the Billionaire's Bed
The Italian's Runaway Cinderella
Maid for the Greek's Ring
Their Dubai Marriage Makeover
Returning for His Ruthless Revenge

Christmas with a Billionaire

The Christmas She Married the Playboy

Visit the Author Profile page
at Harlequin.com for more titles.

Louise Fuller

HER DIAMOND DEAL
WITH THE CEO

PAPL
DISCARDED

HARLEQUIN
PRESENTS

HARLEQUIN®
PRESENTS™

Recycling programs
for this product may
not exist in your area.

ISBN-13: 978-1-335-58456-4

Her Diamond Deal with the CEO

Copyright © 2023 by Louise Fuller

For questions and comments about the quality of this book,
please contact us at CustomerService@Harlequin.com.

Harlequin Enterprises ULC
22 Adelaide St. West, 41st Floor
Toronto, Ontario M5H 4E3, Canada
www.Harlequin.com

Printed in U.S.A.

HER DIAMOND DEAL
WITH THE CEO

CHAPTER ONE

STEADYING HERSELF ON the pale golden sand, Ondine breathed in deeply. Dipper's Beach was too
narrow and steep for the tourists who flocked to
the Florida coastline so, aside from the occasional
crab and the seagulls that stalked the shoreline,
it was almost always deserted.

But she preferred it like that.

It was the first time in nearly three weeks that
she wasn't working so she could have had a lie-in
this morning. Only her brain had jerked awake as
it always did, one minute before her alarm went
off. She could have rolled over and gone back to
sleep, but she loved the early mornings when the
sun was turning the sky above her beach house
shell-pink. It was the one time of day she could
call her own. When she wasn't working.

She squinted upwards. At work, there was
never time to pause or linger. But here on the
beach nobody would be trying to catch her eye
or snapping their fingers. There was just the sun,
the sky and an endless blue sea.

Her gaze narrowed on the shimmering water
framed between the grass-edged dunes.

As a child, she was average at most things but
swimming had been her 'superpower'. The one

thing she'd excelled at in a family of high achievers. Every day she'd trained before school and almost every weekend she'd swum in competitions. Briefly, ludicrously, she'd even imagined herself stepping onto a podium but then she'd got injured and nowadays she swam for pleasure and for her job as a lifeguard at Whitecaps, the exclusive beachside hotel in Palm Beach favoured by the wealthy and beautiful.

Not that she got a chance to use her skills very often.

Unlike the public pool where she'd worked before, most of the Whitecaps residents preferred to lounge by the pool rather than swim in it, and the same was true of the hotel's private stretch of beach.

It was her second year at the hotel and now, as well as being a lifeguard, she worked most evenings as a waitress in the bar and restaurant. Her mouth twisted. She didn't hate either of her jobs; it just wasn't how she'd pictured her life. Two jobs. Two divorces. Living in some rented beach shack—

But the tips were phenomenal, and thanks to Vince, her useless second ex-husband, that mattered more than job satisfaction.

Thinking about the pile of brown envelopes sitting on her kitchen counter, she felt her stomach knot. Sometimes, normally after a particularly exhausting shift, she tried to work out how many glasses she would have to collect before she would be debt-free. Mostly though she was too tired to do anything but eat a bowl of pasta or, more lately, cereal and go to bed.

'*Hola, Ondine. Cómo está hoy?*'

Spinning round, Ondine smiled at the elderly woman with pristine grey hair who was walking towards her. Dolores was her nearest neighbour and even though she was eighty-one years old, she walked her fawn-coloured chihuahua, Hercules, along the beach twice every day.

'Are you swimming today, *chica*? But you have the day off, no?'

'*Hola*, Dolores. Hi, Herc.' She double-kissed the older woman's cheeks, then reached down to stroke the little dog's velvety ears. 'I'm not in until this evening, but I thought I'd get up and have a swim, and now I'm glad I did.' Her eyes tracked down the empty beach. 'It's so beautiful and peaceful today.'

'Not so peaceful last night.' Glancing out to the beautiful white yacht anchored close to the shoreline, Dolores clicked her tongue disapprovingly so that the dog's chin jerked upwards. 'Such noise. Music and shouting. All kinds of goings-on. Some people are so thoughtless.' She sniffed. 'Anyway, you enjoy your swim, *chica*.'

'Thanks, Dolores. See you tomorrow. Bye,

Herc.' She smiled as Dolores waved the chihuahua's tiny paw.

Out at the sea, the yacht danced lightly on the waves.

Once upon a time it might have impressed her, but she worked in Palm Beach. There were as many yachts as there were palm trees.

Unzipping her hoodie, she pushed her shorts down her thighs and kicked off her flip-flops. The sand was like warm sugar and for a moment she just stood there, wiggling her toes. 'That man is richest whose pleasures are cheapest.' That was something her mum used to say but it was hard to feel rich when your kitchen counter was piled high with unpaid bills.

Her feet stilled. She should have kept a closer eye on Vince. She knew he liked to spend money but she hadn't wanted to admit to herself that she had messed up again. Married the wrong man, *again*.

Her eyes fixed on the yacht, her heart thumping heavily against her ribs as she remembered the end of her first marriage. Garrett's infidelity had been humiliating, devastating, but she could have coped, had been coping. Only then, three weeks later, before she had plucked up the courage to tell them she was getting divorced, her parents had died in a car crash.

She shivered in the warm breeze. Overnight,

she had become an orphan, and her fifteen-year-old brother's guardian. She'd moved back to Florida to look after Oliver, and a month later, she'd met Vince at the hardware store. He'd made her laugh and when he'd asked her out, he'd made her laugh again. When he'd taken her out, he'd made her feel sexy.

It was a textbook rebound relationship, but that hadn't stopped her saying *yes* when Vince had proposed. A year later, the marriage had been over, confirming, as if she'd needed further proof, that she was not the marrying kind. This time her pride had taken less of a hit but she'd lost her home, and she was still paying off the credit-card bills.

The one small sliver of silver in the cloud of debt was that Oliver's college fund was tied up in some savings plan. She felt some of the tightness in her chest loosen. Unlike her, Oli knew exactly what he wanted to be and he had the brains and the determination to make it happen. Right now, he was volunteering at an outreach clinic in Costa Rica before he started medical school in September.

She frowned, her gaze snagging on the yacht.

There was someone on deck. Not someone. A man wearing a dark jacket and trousers, his white shirt loose around his throat. She watched as he crouched down and picked up a bottle, shook it and then raised his arm, crooking his elbow as if he was about to hurl it into the sea.

'Don't you dare,' she whispered.

As if he had heard her, the man looked up, and she felt a flicker of something hot and tingling like electricity snap up her spine. He couldn't see her face. She knew that because she couldn't see his, but she could see his powerful body silhouetted against the sky, sunlight clinging to his outline, gilding him in a wash of clear gold like a character in an F. Scott Fitzgerald novel.

The bottle dangled from his fingertips and then he let it fall onto the deck, straightened up and shrugged off his jacket with a conscious carelessness that made her whole body stiffen with dislike and envy.

Her mouth curled into something midway between a sneer and a scowl. It was the same gesture favoured by the hotel's trust-fund-financed clientele when they tossed tips onto the bar or used towels by their loungers.

Picturing their expensive winter tans and inherited Rolexes, she narrowed her eyes on the man as he walked across the deck. And then her pulse jerked as without warning he spun round and took a running jump over the rippling sea. There was a moment of absolute silence as he flew through the air and then he hit the water with an audible splash.

What the—?

She felt her body tense, her hand reaching up automatically for the float over her shoulder. Except it wasn't there because she wasn't at work.

Swearing softly, she moved towards the curling waves at the shoreline. She had spent the whole of spring break watching privileged young men clown around in the water. But did they have to do it when she was off duty?

Eyes fixed on the spot where he had disappeared beneath the waves, she began counting the distance in strokes as the seconds passed.

Surely he should have surfaced by now.

She was running into the sea before her brain understood the implication of that thought, barely registering the water as it splashed over her thighs, and then she was swimming, her body slicing through the surf, eyes scanning the waves, all of her training no longer theoretical but becoming in an instant so real that there was no room for panic or emotion.

What was that?

She saw a flash of gold, and then just as quickly it was gone again.

Breathing in sharply, she ducked beneath the waves, and her heart gave a huge leap forward just as the man had done moments earlier. There he was, his white shirt dazzlingly bright beneath the water, his hands reaching up.

Seconds later she reached him, her arm moved automatically around his chest and she pulled him to the surface, tilting back his head and kicking towards the shoreline. Breathing unsteadily, she dragged him onto the sand and now she saw the front of his shirt was not white but patterned.

No, not patterned. Those were bloodstains.

Over the sound of her heartbeat, she heard the voice of her instructors. *'Always start with your ABCs. Check the airways. Two breaths as soon as the victim is stable in the water or on land, then move into thirty compressions.'*

Her body was shuddering from the swim and the adrenaline but her mind was clear. Sliding two fingers under his chin, she tilted back his head, pinched his nose, put her lips to his mouth and put a breath in, waited then put a second breath in—

The man coughed, and she rolled him onto his side, and he lay there, breathing raggedly, his hand fluttering against the sand.

'It's okay, you're okay.' She squeezed his shoulder. 'You got into trouble, but you're safe now.'

Was he? She stared down at him, her heart beating like a train. The bloodstains looked shockingly vivid against the white cotton and she began unbuttoning his shirt, her hands rough with fear as she checked for injury.

'What are you doing?'

His voice was hoarse from swallowing seawater but hearing him speak cut through her panic and steadied her.

'You have blood on your shirt. I need to—'

He waved his hand dismissively. 'You don't need to worry about that. There was a fight last night, I tried to break it up—' Now he touched his mouth and she saw that there was a cut on his lip that she hadn't noticed before. 'Got punched for my efforts—'

He shivered, his arm dropping to cover his eyes and, frowning, she reached over and grabbed her hoodie and laid it over his chest. 'Should have had you there,' he mumbled. 'You must be pretty strong to pull me out of the water like that.'

'It's my job. I'm a lifeguard.'

So do your job, she told herself, tearing her gaze from his curving mouth. Taking his wrist, she felt his pulse. It was steady, she thought with relief. 'Do you have any alcohol or drugs in your system?'

'What?' He frowned. 'No, nothing—'

Remembering the bottle, she stared down at him uncertainly, but he was breathing and his pulse was firm and they could check him over at the hospital.

'Okay, well, everything is going to be fine. All you need to do is stay where you are. I'm going to go get some help—'

She didn't want to leave him alone but the

chances of help turning up on the beach were slim to none. Her shoulders tensed. If only she had brought her phone, but it was sitting on the kitchen counter.

'No.' His hand clamped around her wrist, surprisingly strong. 'I don't need help. I have help. You're a lifeguard—'

'But I'm not a doctor.' She spoke calmly but firmly as she'd been taught. 'Look, I just live over there. I'm going to run back to my house and call the EMS and they'll come and check you out.'

For a moment she thought he was going to argue. It was a fairly common response. People, men particularly, were often embarrassed at being 'rescued' but medical opinion on the protocol for post-near-drownings was clear. Anyone requiring any form of resuscitation needed to be evaluated by a healthcare provider, even if they appeared alert with good breathing and a strong pulse.

'Fine. Whatever.' He let go of her arm, waving his hand in the same dismissive way as before.

Reaching for her shorts, she pulled them on and got to her feet. 'I'll be five minutes, tops. Just sit tight and try not to worry. It really is just precautionary. My name is Ondine, by the way.'

'Jack.' He shifted back against the sand, his eyes still closed. 'Jack Walcott.'

I know who you are.

She almost spoke the words out loud and her face felt suddenly hot.

Jack Walcott was the heir to the Walcott energy empire. He was also a guest at Whitecaps. In a hotel filled with beautiful, indolent people, he was the most beautiful. A baby-faced billionaire with dirty-blond hair, eyes the colour of pirate gold and a face of such absurdly perfect proportions and symmetry that it was hard not to simply stare and keep on staring.

And he knew it.

How could he not? Jack Walcott was moviestar-gorgeous with a smile that could tip the planet into meltdown.

Her mouth thinned. He was also hedonistic, self-indulgent and arrogant. Lolling on a lounger in a pair of plain blue swim shorts designed to highlight his smooth gold skin and curving muscles, he had looked straight through her. And on the days when he'd eaten in the restaurant, he hadn't so much as glanced up from his steak when she'd brought him the mustard he'd requested. To him, she was just staff. One of the many minions paid to meet his every need.

But he would have to be in a trance or unconscious not to notice the effect he had on people. How they craned their necks to watch him walk by, elbowed their neighbours, whispered behind their hands.

Her eyes dropped irresistibly to the contoured lines of his stomach, and now she didn't just want to stare, she wanted to touch, stroke, scratch—

She felt her fingers twitch and, aware of the impropriety of her response, she clamped her hands tightly to her hips and got to her feet.

'I'll be right back, Jack,' she said quickly. His eyes stayed shut.

She ran across the sand and was halfway up the dunes when something made her look back over her shoulder to check on him. Her mouth fell open. Jack Walcott was not where she'd left him. He wasn't even lying down. He was walking along the beach, her hoodie draped across his shoulders, moving with a slow, languid grace that made her feel light-headed. Swearing under her breath, she ran back towards him.

'Hey—'

He turned, his blond hair flopping across his forehead. His shirt was almost dry now so that instead of sticking to his skin it was lifting in the breeze, revealing even more of the spectacular body beneath. She glared up into his face to stop herself from looking.

'Haven't you forgotten something?'

His eyes narrowed into the sunlight.

'Oh, yeah, my bad. Here.' The gold signet ring on his little finger glinted as he unpeeled her hoodie from around his shoulders and draped it over hers.

'That's not what I meant,' she snapped, and now finally he looked at her. Really looked at her in a way that made her feel suddenly and intensely conscious of herself, of the rise and fall of her breasts, the heavy thud of her heart, the tightness of her skin.

The gold of his eyes was steady but then something rippled beneath the flawless features, like the tremors that preceded an earthquake, almost as if he could feel her reaction, as if he was feeling it too—

Afterwards, she would wonder who made the first move. Perhaps he leaned forward or maybe she lost her footing but one moment she was glaring up at him, the next their lips were brushing and there was an emptiness in her stomach like hunger, only it was a hunger she had never felt.

His mouth was soft and warm and teasing and, dissolving with desire, she felt his hand slide round her waist and then heat was seeping through her limbs so that it was impossible not to melt against him, unthinkable not to press her body against the hard muscles of his chest.

His lips parted hers, stirring her, and she kissed him back, tasting salt and a hunger that matched her own and all the while her body was melting, her defences softening—

She breathed in sharply, and, heart hammering, she stumbled backwards. 'What the hell do you think you're doing?'

It was a good question, particularly because it meant that she didn't have to ask herself what she was doing kissing someone she had just pulled out of the sea. 'You can't just go around kissing people.'

Tilting back his head, he looked down at her. 'To be fair, you kissed me first,' he said softly.

'What I did was give you CPR. Now what are you doing?' she said breathlessly as he began backing away from her.

'I'm going back to my hotel.'

'No, you're not.' With an effort, she fought to keep her voice under control. 'You shouldn't be going anywhere, particularly on your own. That's why I told you to stay where you were.'

He shrugged. 'I got bored.'

Bored?

She could feel her nostrils flaring, and her heart was banging hard against her ribs. 'You need to see a doctor.'

'I am.' He frowned. 'Or rather I was.' He stared down at her, his beautiful mouth changing shape again, the corners curving up into a mocking smile that made her heart beat painfully fast. 'As of last night, I'm pretty sure I'm single again.'

She spoke without thinking. 'If you treat your

partners with as little respect as you do your own welfare, I can't say I'm surprised.'

He stared at her in silence.

'Is that right?' The smile had vanished. 'I thought you said I needed a doctor, not a psychiatrist.' He made another of those dismissive gestures; he seemed to have an endless supply of them at his fingertips. 'Look, I'm sure you mean well, Odette, but I'm really tired, and right now I don't need a lecture, I just want to go to bed.' As if to prove his point, he yawned, extending his arms above his head, his spine curving like a cat.

'It's Ondine not Odette, and right now, you shouldn't be on your own,' she said stiffly.

His eyes were looking directly into hers. 'In bed?'

She felt her cheeks grow hot. In fact, her whole body felt as if it were on fire.

'I couldn't agree more.' The gleam in his eyes made the air leave her lungs. 'Are you offering to join me?' The mocking smile dented his cheek again. 'If so, we should probably go back to your place. It's closer.'

'I'm not offering to join you, and there is no "we",' she snapped.

He tilted his head back. 'I'm just messing with you—'

'Because this isn't a big enough mess?' She glared at him. 'You might feel fine now, but lung complications are surprisingly common after near-drownings. Chemical imbalances can develop, irregular heart rhythms can occur—'

'Okay, okay.' He held up his hands. 'I get it. But you don't need to call an ambulance. I have a car at the hotel. I can drive myself.'

Fighting an urge to roll her eyes, she shook her head. 'No, you can't.' And he probably wouldn't, she thought, remembering how he had walked off down the beach the moment she had turned her back. 'Which is why I'm going to take you myself.'

He was frowning down at her, his eyes searching her face almost as if she had suddenly started speaking gibberish. 'Why would you do that?'

'I told you. You need to see a doctor, and I don't trust you to do the right thing,'

'Impressive,' he said softly. 'It usually takes people way longer to work that out about me.'

Their eyes met and, ignoring the lurch of her pulse, she said, 'You need some shoes. We can pick some up at the house. And I'll grab my phone. Then you can call whoever you need to call to tell them you're okay. It's this way.' And without waiting, she turned and stalked away across the sand.

Five minutes later they were juddering along the road in her old in-need-of-a-clean Honda Civic. Beside her, Jack filled his chair; filled the entire car, all long muscular legs and square shoulders.

'If I didn't need to go to the hospital before, I will now,' he grumbled, wincing as she accelerated past a pizza delivery scooter. 'This feels like I'm riding a jet ski on dry land.'

'It needs new shock absorbers,' she said crisply. 'But you won't have to put up with it for long.' There were four hospitals within driving distance of her house, but she knew without asking which one to take him to. Solace Health was the private medical centre favoured by the rich and famous. There were orchids on the reception desk and, instead of disinfectant, it smelled of orange blossom and money.

'Do you mean the Solace?' He frowned. 'Isn't there another hospital?'

'Yes, but they're further away. And they're not private, which means there'll be more people there. Which means you'll have to wait,' she added, when he didn't react.

He shrugged. 'I don't mind waiting.'

She stared at him impatiently, remembering the imperious way he clicked his fingers at the poolside, but before she could respond he reached over and plucked her sunglasses from her nose and slid them in front of his eyes. She blinked as his fingers grazed her cheek. His touch was as light as the grass that brushed against her bare legs out on the dunes, only the grass never made her skin grow hot and tight.

'I'd rather wait than go to the Solace.' He frowned. 'They know me there. Know my family. I don't need any more drama.'

That she could believe, she thought, as they returned to the car an hour later.

She had told herself that it was his money and air of entitlement that made people react to him as they did, but, slouched against the reception desk in borrowed flip-flops and with half his face hidden behind her sunglasses, Jack Walcott had still created a stir. There was something about him that had made the air in the waiting room shiver with anticipation.

The doctor, a tired-looking man with greying hair, had given Jack the all-clear. But then he'd turned to Ondine and said, 'You need to keep an eye on your husband, Mrs Walcott. He needs rest but I would sit with him while he sleeps. Any difficulties in breathing, change in colour or if it's hard to wake him up, come straight back in.'

'She will—won't you, honey?' Jack had said, his eyes gleaming. 'She's a great wife. I'm a very lucky man.'

She should have corrected him but instead she'd found herself nodding. 'Yes, I can do that.'

'I'll drop you back at Whitecaps,' she said now,

reversing out of the space. 'You have someone there who can keep an eye on you, don't you?'

His eyes rested on her face. 'How do you know where I'm staying?'

She swore silently but there was no way to backtrack. 'I work there,' she said finally, looking up to meet his gaze. 'I recognised you.'

He leaned back, his pupils flaring. 'I thought you seemed familiar.' His forehead creased. It gave him a puppyish air that she found immensely irritating. Or rather she found it irritating the way her body responded.

'I'm one of the lifeguards,' she said stiffly. 'You probably saw me at the pool or the beach.' Hands tightening around the wheel, she turned into the oncoming traffic. 'Or maybe in the restaurant.'

'They have lifeguards in the restaurant. Wow!' He raised one eyebrow. 'Those soup bowls must be deeper than they look.'

He didn't need any encouragement, she knew that, and she tried to stop herself from smiling but her mouth had a mind of its own and she felt it curve upwards despite her wishes.

'I work as a waitress too. In the evenings.'

'So when do you get time off?'

It was a simple question but he made it feel complicated. Flustered, she said, 'Now. This is my day off.' And instantly regretted it as his gold eyes fixed on her face, curious and assessing.

'And you decided to spend it with me. I'm flattered.'

'Don't be,' she said quickly, pressing the air conditioning button with fingers that were suddenly shaky and incompetent. 'I'd do the same for anyone.'

That was true, she told herself firmly, only she could feel colour creeping over her cheeks and collarbone. Worse, she knew that Jack could see what she was feeling, but there was nothing she could do about that.

'If you say so,' he murmured. He shifted back against his seat, stretching out his legs. 'So why do you have two jobs? Seems very greedy. I mean, I don't even have one.'

There was an edge beneath the languid drawl she didn't understand but then she didn't want to understand Jack Walcott. Nor, more importantly, did he need to understand her.

She shrugged. 'I have a lot of outgoings.'

That was the short answer. The longer, more humiliating version was that she had let an idiot be in charge of her money. But she wasn't about to share that particular fact with Jack Walcott.

'Why not focus on one job, and get promoted?' He tipped his head back, letting the sun fall across his face. 'Or you could marry the boss,' he said, pushing her glasses back along his nose.

She glared at him. Spoken like a man who

didn't need to earn a living. 'How wonderfully progressive of you. But I don't want to marry my boss.' She didn't want to marry anyone. She'd made the same mistake twice. She didn't need to do it again. 'Besides, marriage only works for men.'

'Not this man.' His fingers tapped out a rhythm against the door seal. 'I like my freedom.'

'I'm sure you do. I'm just saying that statistically marriage is good for men. They live longer. And they earn more because people think they're more dedicated, responsible, mature.'

Clearly they hadn't met her ex-husbands, she thought, flipping the indicator stalk up with unnecessary force.

'You mean, even when they're none of those things?'

Jack was looking at her. His eyes were shielded by her sunglasses but she could feel his focus.

'I suppose, yes.'

'So how does flip-flop man fit into that?'

'Who?' She glanced over at him, frowning, momentarily distracted from the traffic.

'The guy whose shoes I'm wearing.'

She had forgotten all about the flip-flops. 'Oh, those…they belong to my little brother. He lives with me.'

'Little?' He raised an eyebrow.

'I meant little in age, not size.'

Thinking about Oliver, she felt some of the tension of the morning drop from her body. He had been taller than her since he was thirteen years old. Now, at nineteen, he was six feet two, broad and handsome like their dad but with their mother's smile. He was the one good thing in her life. The one thing she hadn't messed up.

'How does your boyfriend feel about living with your kid brother?'

She felt her body still. There was one of two ways she could answer that question. Tell him the truth, which was that she was single. Or tell him that it was none of his business, but if she did that he would think she was single anyway.

'I don't have a boyfriend.' His blond hair was fluttering in the breeze and she tried to make her voice sound as casual as he looked. Oliver was the only man in her life right now, and, given her track record with men, it would be safer for it to stay that way.

'But as we're discussing partners, there is going to be someone who can sit with you while you sleep—'

'Isn't that your turn?'

'What? No—'

Caught off guard, she glanced towards him, shaking her head, but he was already reaching over to take hold of the steering wheel, jerking it left into the oncoming traffic. There was a blaring, overlapping eruption of horns.

'What is wrong with you?' She pushed his hand from the wheel. 'Do you have some sort of death wish?'

'You were going the wrong way.'

'The hotel is in that direction,' she snapped.

'Yeah, about that.' Flopping back in his seat, he screwed up his face. 'I could do with keeping this little episode off the radar so I was thinking I might come back to yours.'

CHAPTER TWO

SERIOUSLY?

Slamming her foot on the brakes, Ondine turned sharply to face him. 'Come back to mine?'

She could see her distorted reflection in the lens of her sunglasses, and irritably she reached over and snatched them from his face.

'Calm down,' he protested. 'I didn't mean it like that—'

A vivid image of what 'that' might look like with Jack popped into her head and she blinked it away. In the rear-view mirror, she could see the driver behind them mouthing something. 'Don't tell me to calm down—'

'I'm sorry.' Jack leaned forward, his golden eyes fixing on her face. 'I just don't want to go back to Whitecaps looking like this.' He gestured towards his bloodstained shirt. 'They're no different from the Solace. Someone will call my grandfather and I don't need him getting upset.'

Behind them, the driver had decided to reiterate his frustration by pressing his horn repeatedly. She watched Jack turn, a muscle pulsing in his cheek, and abruptly the hooting stopped.

'Look, I know I was a jerk earlier, and you probably want to get shot of me, but I really need somewhere to sleep for a couple of hours. On my own, just to be clear,' he added.

Ondine stared at him, her hands tightening around the steering wheel to steady herself. He was right. She did want to get shot of him. Because Jack Walcott was a dare and a temptation all wrapped up like the most beautiful present under a Christmas tree. And because she could still feel the imprint of his mouth on hers. Only where would he go if she said no?

As if sensing her weakness, he locked eyes with hers. 'Please, Ondine.'

For a few, unravelling seconds, her heart clenched. It was the first time he had used her name, and for some reason it sounded different when he said it. He made her feel different.

She gritted her teeth. He wasn't her responsibility. There was nothing in the American Lifeguard Association training programme to prepare her for having a man like Jack Walcott in her house. But there was a tension in his voice, a strain that wrenched at something inside her so that she heard herself say, 'Fine. You can come back to my house. *To sleep.* And it's just for a couple of hours.'

'Thank you,' he said softly.

She could do this, she thought as the car moved

forward. It was just a couple of hours, and then Jack would leave and life would go back to how it was before.

As soon as he lay down on the bed, Jack fell asleep.

He slept, and he dreamed only it didn't feel like dreaming. It felt as though he were still awake, and he were on the yacht again, turning to run and jump, only Ondine was frowning at him in that precise, focused way of hers, her blue eyes steadying him as she took his wrist and felt for his pulse and then her hands were sliding over his shoulders, mouth fitting against his, warm and soft and—

Rolling onto his back, he blinked open his eyes.

The curtains were drawn but there was a gap the width of a tie and he could see the sun hanging high in the sky like an orange waiting to be picked and squeezed.

Feeling suddenly thirsty, he sat up, his gaze moving slowly around the room.

Aside from its tidiness, which was probably due to the absence of its usual occupant, it was a typical teenage boy's bedroom. Miami Dolphins posters were tacked to the wall. There was a desktop computer with a bunch of games piled up beside it and a life-size replica skeleton dangled from the ceiling. Left over from Halloween, he thought as the curtains lifted in the breeze.

His eyes moved to the bookshelves, skimming over the sci-fi novels and academic textbooks to lock onto a framed photo. He stared at it for a moment, feeling his body tense, and then he got to his feet and reached over to pick it up.

He scanned the faces intently. There was no doubt who they were. Mum. Dad. Oliver. And Ondine. His fingers tightened against the glass. They were on one of those log-flume rides, the kind where you meandered along a waterway, rising up a hill before dropping at speed. The photo had been taken seconds after splashdown and their eyes were wide with shock and the thrill of it.

They looked happy.

They looked like a family.

He stared down at the photo, envy cut through with a twist of bitterness filling his gut. He had a family, two really since his parents' divorce and yet he wasn't a part of either of them. And he felt the misery and the shame of it rush over his head, pulling him under—

His gaze snagged on Ondine's face and he could almost feel the grip of her hand on his shoulder. She was strong, stronger than she looked. She had confidence in her body too as if she trusted it to do what she wanted it to. And once she had agreed to let him stay, she had been as calm and pragmatic as she had been on the beach and at the hospital, he thought, remembering how she had shown him into her brother's bedroom.

'You need to sleep.' She reached past him and folded back the duvet. 'You're exhausted.'

'What are you doing?' he asked as she dragged an old rattan armchair across the room.

'I'm keeping an eye on you.' Picking up a paperback book from the bedside table, she sat down, frowning at the cover.

'You don't have to do that.'

She gave a delicate shrug. 'I told the doctor I would.'

Their eyes met, hers wide and wary; he could see her pulse hammering against the pale, thin skin of her throat and he knew that she was remembering the moment in the hospital when he told that same doctor she was his wife.

'And you always do what you say you will.'

It wasn't a question, but she acted as if it were. 'Yes. If I say I'm going to do something, I do it.'

'For better, for worse, Mrs Walcott,' he murmured as he lay down.

Her expression shifted briefly, her face contracting or retreating in a way he couldn't put a finger on, but then that smile curved her mouth and she sat back in the chair and opened the book. 'Go to sleep, Jack.'

He had no memory of his eyes closing, but he could remember Ondine sitting in the armchair, the book in her hand.

But the chair was empty now. He felt a ripple of anger scud across his skin, and a disappointment that felt disproportionate. What happened to 'if I say I'm going to do something, I do it'?

His shoulders tensed. But should he really be that surprised? Plenty of people, people who had a far stronger duty of care for him than Ondine, had made promises they couldn't or wouldn't keep.

When it came to him anyway.

Only his grandfather had ever followed through. Chivvying him, coaxing him, *caring*. Abruptly, he put the frame down on the shelf, and as he did so he spotted it. A piece of paper, folded in half, with his name written in block capitals.

He picked it up and opened it.

Just popped out to get some milk. Back soon. Don't wander off. O

O.

He could see Ondine's mouth forming the shape of the letter just as it had on the beach when he'd draped the hoodie over her shoulders and suddenly his skin was prickling again.

Was that why he had kissed her? That mouth.

He frowned, his mind liquid, the memory swelling and changing direction like a raindrop sliding down a windowpane. Or had she kissed him?

Not that it mattered.

Ondine wasn't his type. Too serious, too snitty, plus she was seriously bossy, he thought, remembering how she had more or less frogmarched him into the medical centre. Looks-wise, her hair was a fairly boring mid-brown, her cheekbones a little too pronounced, and those startlingly blue eyes seemed to be permanently narrowed in his direction so that he shouldn't have found her beautiful and yet—

That mouth.

Great legs too. A pulse of heat danced across his skin as he remembered her toned calf muscles, that smooth skin.

He blinked the memory away. For him, that kiss was about the moment, not the woman. He had just nearly drowned; he'd needed to feel the warmth of breath, the firmness of lips, the pulse of life beating through him. And lust, desire, hunger, whatever name you gave it, was the opposite of those tenuous, liminal moments beneath the water. It was a sure thing, a talisman, as solid and real as any lifebelt.

And the reason his skin was tingling now when he thought about it was because of the salt. All he needed to do was shower and it would be as if nothing had ever happened.

The bathroom was next door. It was small—the elevator in his Manhattan apartment was larger— but the shower itself was surprisingly spacious, and there was a pile of clean towels folded on top of a wicker laundry basket.

Stripping off, he took a breath and stepped under the shower head, keeping the jet of water trained on his back.

He should have just stayed in the bar. He hadn't felt like partying and he hated boats. But everyone had wanted to go on the yacht. Plus, Carrie had stormed off by then and he hated being on his own more. If he was on his own then all those thoughts he usually had no trouble keeping at bay would come creeping out of the dark corners. Thoughts that made it impossible to sit still, because whenever you sat still they crept up and smothered you like a fog.

When he was a child everyone thought he had ADHD, and it was true that he shared some of the symptoms. But for him, it was elective. To keep moving was to keep one step ahead. He took risks too, like today. Stupid, pointless risks that flooded his body and brain with adrenaline. And if that wasn't an option then he partied because surrounding himself with people, acting as if he didn't care about what they or anyone else thought, made it easier to not think about his parents' rejection.

Except he did care what his grandfather thought.

Picking up the soap, he rubbed it over the muscles of his chest, feeling his heartbeat beneath his fingertips.

The world knew John D. Walcott IV as an oil tycoon. The man who had turned a moderate family business into a household brand. A global company for the modern world. But to him, he was just Grandpa. Always there, always firm but fair; kind, tolerant, endlessly patient.

Until two months ago. When his patience had abruptly run out.

Even now he could picture the look of disappointment on his grandfather's familiar, lined face. And it was his fault.

Having come out of yet another meeting where his suggested investment in a renewables project had been long-grassed, he was feeling thwarted and frustrated at the Walcott Energy Corporation's snail's-pace transition to greener energy and so was careless and impatient, skim-reading a geological report rather than giving it the forensic attention it deserved before signing off on the deal.

Naturally, because not all the people employed by WEC were related to his grandfather, and therefore didn't have the luxury of letting their frustrations affect their work, the issue was spotted but by then it was too late. The paperwork was being processed and so the Canadians had to be paid off in order to terminate the deal.

To add insult to injury, when the proverbial hit the fan, he was partying in Turks and Caicos.

It was the last and very final straw for John D. Walcott IV.

He summoned his eldest grandchild to the WEC head office and told him bluntly that he needed to grow up. And that until he could demonstrate the maturity expected of an heir in waiting, the position of CEO was no longer his by birthright. As of immediate effect he was to step down from the board and clear his desk. His newly expanded free time should be spent evaluating his life, his lifestyle and his future.

Jack stared down at the water swirling into the plughole.

He had been shocked, disbelieving at first, then angry, but above all else it had hurt, and far more than he could have imagined, to experience such cool objectivity where he had only been used to indulgent affection. After everything that had happened with his parents, he hadn't known he could still feel, still care, but he did, the more so because it was his fault, and because he hated knowing that he had let his grandfather down.

Of course his grandpa couldn't stay angry for long—

But disappointment was not the same as anger. His grandfather loved him but that didn't mean he trusted him. To become the next CEO, he was going to have to earn back that trust. Prove he could change. Make his grandfather proud.

His mouth twisted. So last night he had partied on a yacht, broken up with the woman he'd been seeing, and then jumped into the sea and nearly drowned.

Perfect. Good job, Jack!

He tipped his face up unthinkingly and water spilled into his eyes and he jerked away, his heart suddenly racing as he remembered the moment when the sea closed over his head. Breathing out unsteadily, he pressed the palms of his hands against the tiles, steadying his heartbeat, steadying himself as all the possible consequences of his actions slammed into him like a rogue wave.

Jumping off a yacht into the sea was by far the stupidest thing he'd ever done. Given that he couldn't swim, it was not just stupid but insanely dangerous.

He shivered. Except it hadn't felt dangerous at

the time, just necessary. Seeing that photo of his mother with his half-brother, Penn, had made the familiar numbness start. He had felt himself disappearing and he had needed something to pull him back, something to fill the gap inside his chest. And so he'd jumped into the sea.

And the stupid thing was he had actually forgotten that he couldn't swim. Or maybe not forgotten. It was more that it seemed implausible that was still true. That he hadn't simply learned by some kind of osmosis from all the people around him who could swim.

His stomach twisted painfully as he remembered the weight of the water, and the taste of fear in his mouth and his heartbeat filling his head—

Blanking his mind, he switched off the shower, dried himself and got dressed before making his way back to Oliver's bedroom. If only he had some actual shoes, he thought, sliding his feet back into the flip-flops, but at least his clothes were dry now, and the bloodstain on his shirt looked less vividly red.

'Good. You're awake.'

The light, husky voice knocked his train of thought off course and he turned. Ondine was standing in the doorway.

He felt his pulse change lanes and accelerate.

She had changed clothes. Now she was wearing a simple cotton dress that managed to both cover and reveal the shape of her body and even though he had told himself earlier that she wasn't his type, he had to make a conscious effort not to stare at her.

'I took a shower. You don't mind, do you?'

'Of course not. I left some towels out for you. And I thought you might want something to drink.' There was a glass of water in one hand and, judging by the steam spiralling upwards, a mug of something hot in the other.

'I didn't know what you like so I brought water and coffee. You should drink the water anyway,' she added, handing out both.

He screwed up his face. 'Didn't I drink enough earlier?'

It was the first time either of them had referred to what happened and even though he had done so obliquely he felt the shock of it ripple through him.

'Yes, but that was salt water, so you need to rehydrate.' The careful neutrality of her voice matched the level expression on her face but there was a flicker of concern in her eyes. 'Do you have a headache? Any dizziness?'

Glancing down at the glass of water, he felt his stomach lurch, the moment when the sea had started to pull him down suddenly suffocatingly vivid inside his head.

'No, nothing. But I might start with the coffee first.'

He could no longer smell the salt on his skin but every time he breathed in, he could still taste the sea. Picking up the cup, he let the hot liquid scour his mouth and then he put the cup and the glass on the desk.

'He's studying medicine, isn't he? Your brother, I mean. How far along is he?'

She stared at him, her blue gaze level and assessing. *Unimpressed.* 'He hasn't started yet. He's on a gap year, doing medical outreach work in Costa Rica.' There was a brief silence, her obvious desire to keep her private life private vying with her curiosity. He felt a flicker of satisfaction as her curiosity won. 'How did you know he was studying medicine?'

'Elementary, my dear Mrs Walcott,' he said softly, his pulse skipping a beat as her eyes narrowed a fraction. 'The chemistry and biology textbooks, the cuddly chromosome—' leaning forward, he picked up the purple plush toy '—and of course our undernourished friend.' He gave the skeleton a gentle push. 'Where's he going?'

'Stanford.' A flush of colour seeped over her cheekbones. He could hear the pride in her voice and something pinched inside his chest. He couldn't imagine anyone sounding that way when they talked about him. Not even his grandfather.

At least not right now.

'Must be a smart kid.' Picking up his coffee, he took another sip. Ouch, he thought, wincing as the hot liquid made contact with the graze on his lip.

Her eyes arrowed in on his face. 'Do you want some antiseptic cream for that?'

He shook his head. 'I just need to be more careful.'

One fine dark eyebrow arched upwards. 'Sounds like a plan. So, what was the fight about?'

The fight? For a moment, he stared at her blankly. He had forgotten telling her that detail. Now, thinking back to it was like looking into the wrong end of a telescope. It seemed tiny and distant and unimportant.

'It was nothing—'

The evening had started well enough. They had gone to Blackjacks, and everyone had been dancing and drinking whisky sours. Everyone except him. He had wanted to, needed to, but that need had given him the willpower to stay on the soft drinks.

Only then Harry had pulled out some pills.

His shoulders tensed. He still wasn't entirely sure why, given that he had neither brought the drugs or taken them, but Harry's girlfriend, Lizzie, had got completely out of shape with him, kicking off about his 'attitude' and his 'behaviour', both of which were apparently substandard. To add insult to injury, Carrie had got involved. He couldn't remember every word but the gist of it was he was irresponsible, selfish, made poor life choices and she pitied his mother.

The tension in his shoulders spread down his spine. Even just hearing his mother mentioned had been enough to punch a hole through his chest.

That was when he'd known it was time to end things.

He felt Ondine's gaze on his face, and he tilted his head back to meet her eyes.

'Harry said something stupid about Sam's girlfriend, Maeve, and he should have just apologised but we'd all been partying pretty hard, and he was stoned, and Sam tried to hit Harry, but he punched me by mistake and the drinks went everywhere, and Maeve lost it completely and she ended up telling Harry's girlfriend Lizzie that he'd hooked up with some waitress last week—'

In other words, a fairly average night out. Only for some reason, the whole thing sounded appallingly silly and self-indulgent. He felt suddenly exhausted, as if he hadn't slept at all, and there was a weave of tension pulling his chest tight. To shake it off, he glanced over at Ondine and gave her a small, conspiratorial smile. 'Wasn't you, was it?'

She didn't laugh. Nor did she look upset or annoyed. Just stern.

'Excuse me?'

He held up his hands as he had done out on the beach. 'It was a joke.'

'A joke? You think lying to people is funny.' Two red spots of colour were burning high on her cheekbones.

Lying? He frowned. Maybe he had skimmed the truth but— 'I didn't lie.'

Her chin came up. 'I asked you at the beach and you said you hadn't taken anything. You told the doctor the same thing. Now you're telling me you'd all been "partying pretty hard".'

He felt a sting of impatience, and frustration at the injustice of her accusation. 'First off, Little Miss War-on-Drugs, who made you judge and jury? Secondly, I wasn't lying. I hadn't taken anything. Not that it's any of your business.'

'Right. That's why you jumped into the sea fully clothed, was it?'

Her eyes were the same clear blue as the ocean, and he silently replayed the moment of impact and the accompanying head rush of relief at having something real to fight for even as his thoughts flinched at the memory. It was an act of dark folly. But he had thought he was alone, and he didn't like knowing that she had seen him at his most desperate.

'You lied about that too,' she said coldly. 'You said you were messing about on deck but I saw what happened. Oh, and by the way, it is my business if I have to go fish you out of the ocean.' She shook her head. 'Let me give you a piece of advice, Jack. Next time you want to "mess about", stick to something that doesn't end with a trip to the hospital.'

He'd had enough.

'Seriously? You think I need advice from some waitress-cum-lifeguard?'

She blinked and her face stilled, and he felt her reaction as if it were his own, but his head was still spinning with shock that she knew what he'd done and that drove him to push aside any restraint or consideration.

'Maybe you need to take a good, hard look at how, where you live? Because what I think is that you should get your own life on track before you start picking holes in mine.'

She took a step backwards, and he knew he had gone too far, pushed back too hard as he always did. Even if she hadn't been inching towards the door, he could sense her withdrawing from him, and all of the certainty he'd felt as she'd waited with him at the hospital and sat by his bed began to melt away—

'Ondine, don't go.' His fists tightened, a nameless panic swamping him, pulling him under. 'Please. I don't know why I said that. I didn't mean it—'

Ondine stopped. Her legs seemed to be rooted to the floorboards she and Oli had painted when they moved in. Her eyes were fixed on Jack's face.

He looked pale and his hair was still damp from the shower, just as it had been when she'd pulled him from the sea. And maybe that triggered some kind of reflex need to help and comfort him or maybe it was the strain in his voice, but she knew she couldn't leave him. 'I'm not going anywhere,' she said quietly.

He sat down on the bed abruptly, almost as if his legs had given way, and she realised that the shock of the morning was finally setting in.

Or more likely he had been in shock the whole time. She felt a stab of guilt. She had wanted to believe he was unaffected because that meant she could keep her distance. Now though she saw that the fleeting glimpse of his own mortality had scared him.

And her, she thought, her heart jerking into her ribs. It felt as if her breath and her heartbeat were pushing into one another inside her chest. Her skin could hardly hold it all in.

'Here, drink this. It will help.' She handed him his coffee, hesitated then sat down beside him. 'Is there anyone I can call?'

He looked up at her. 'Call?'

She hesitated again. 'You said you were seeing someone. A doctor.'

'It wasn't that serious. Not for me anyway, and it's over now.' He ran a hand wearily over his face.

'Your parents, then.'

Now, he was shaking his head. 'I don't need to call anyone. I'm fine.'

He wasn't. She could see that now. It had just taken longer for him to react. She stared down at him, wondering why that was. 'Physically yes, but maybe you need to talk to someone about what happened.'

'Then I can talk to you, can't I?'

The strain was still there, and she hesitated again, then took his hand. 'Of course you can talk to me. But there are professionals—'

He was shaking his head. 'But you were there. With me.'

In the shiver of a heartbeat, she remembered her burning lungs, his heavy body. She felt his hand tighten around hers and knew that he was remembering it too.

'Only you know what happened. What it felt like. Just you and me—'

Their eyes met. Through the window she could

see the sun, hear the screech of the gulls, but all of it came from another place, far away. Here it was just the two of them and this relentless pull of need between them that she could no more ignore than the tide could ignore the moon.

He was so beautiful.

Reaching up, she touched his face, her fingers following the curve of his jaw. Her pulse was raging like thunder inside her head.

'Just you and me,' she whispered and then she leaned in and kissed him.

His lips were warm and firm and their mouths fitted together just as they had before, just as if they had kissed not once but a hundred, a thousand times.

Only it was nothing like that first kiss. That had been exploratory, impulsive, organic. This was an admission of that narrow-eyed quivering creature that had been prowling around them and nipping at their heels since they'd left the hospital. It was a kiss of heat and hunger, hers and his.

She felt his hand slide around her waist, and he was pulling her onto his lap, his expression shuttered, his eyes intent on her face.

'No, not here,' she managed. 'My room.'

They moved as one, off the bed and out of the door, bodies colliding off the walls in the urgency of their haste. In the few steps it took to reach her bedroom, their mouths fused again only now, instead of her kissing him, he was kissing her, pushing her dress away from her shoulders, lifting her hair away from her neck, sucking and licking her shoulder, her throat—

His hands moved to her back, to the catch of her bra. Flicking it open, he slid it down her arms and tossed it to the floor and now his hands were cupping her breasts, his thumbs brushing against the nipples so that a moan of pleasure escaped her lips—

Finding her mouth, he kissed her deeply, urgently, his breath melting into hers, but it wasn't enough and she found the button on his waistband, jerking it open, freeing him and she heard his breath snap in his throat as her fingers wrapped around the smooth, hard length of him.

'Wait…wait!' he said hoarsely, his hand gripping her wrist. 'I don't have anything on me—'

'It's okay,' she cut him off. 'I have some.'

Was that true? It had been so long since she had needed to use contraception. Not since with Garrett before they were married. But she didn't want to think about that now. Heart thundering, she yanked open a drawer. Then another. They must be here—

Thank goodness. A rush of relief flooded her as she found the box and then she almost dropped it as his hands slid under the hem of her dress and he pulled her panties down over her thighs. And now he was turning her to face him, his fingers firm, compelling, pulling her with him onto the bed, his mouth hot against hers as she tore clumsily at the wrapper.

'Let me—'

He took the condom from her shaking hands and she watched, dry-mouthed, as he slid it onto his erection. He lifted her up so that her thighs were straddling his hips and now he slowed as he pushed inside her, taking his time, making her wait, letting her register every smooth, pulsing inch of him.

She put her hand on his arm to steady herself as he began to move against her, his hips lifting her up in a hard, intoxicating rhythm that made her head spin. Now he was touching her clitoris, working in time with his thrusts, and she sucked in a breath as his lips found the hollow below her ear.

Her fingers flexed against his warm, bare chest. She was melting, dissolving into a molten pool of need and, reaching up, she clasped his face in her hands, suddenly desperate, her mouth finding his as he rocked faster, and faster and then she cried out, back arching, breath shuddering.

Moments later, a heartbeat at most, he caught her wrists, gripping them tightly and then his lips parted and he was groaning against her mouth, body tensing as he surged inside her.

She felt his hand in her hair and, breathing hard, he fell back on the bed, taking her with him.

Head spinning, she shifted against the white heat of Jack's body. She could feel the sweat on her skin. Their sweat. But it was her face that felt as if it were on fire.

What had she done? But it was a rhetorical question. She knew what she'd done. She'd had sex with Jack Walcott. Or to put it another way, she'd made the biggest mistake of her life. Okay, maybe not the biggest, she thought, catching sight of her ring finger.

But this was definitely a mistake.

He was in the corner of her vision and she turned her head slightly until she could no longer see him. But now she could see the clothes scattered all over the floor where he had pulled them from her greedy, reckless body—

As casually as she could manage, she wriggled out of his arms.

'Where are you going?' His hand moved over her thigh, and she knew that if she let it stay there she would soon be incapable of rational thought.

'I'm just going to use the bathroom.' Sliding her legs off the bed, she stood up so quickly that she almost toppled over. 'I'll leave you to get dressed and...' She let the sentence teeter and fall into the silence between them and, snatching up her clothes, she darted out of the room.

She shut and locked the door.

Gripping the edge of the sink, she stared at her reflection. What was wrong with her? Why did she keep making the same dumb mistakes? Her fingers trembled against the cool porcelain. Since her second divorce had come through she had been single, and if not happy then focused on Oli's future and clearing the debts Vince had racked up in their names. Sex and men were off the agenda for the very simple reason that she couldn't trust herself. And it had been surprisingly easy to resist temptation.

Only then Jack had been there, his golden eyes melting into hers, his face so beautiful it made her ache, and that hard, lean body promising every kind of pleasure. Mouth dry, she stared into her reflected eyes, pressing her thighs tight. And not just promising. He had delivered.

Probably because he'd had so much practice, she thought, picturing her own shaking hands as she'd tried to unwrap the condom.

She felt her cheeks grow warm. Her lack of expertise was embarrassing to remember but at least she'd had some condoms left over, because truthfully she'd been so caught up in her hunger for him that she couldn't say for sure if she would have done something unforgivably stupid in the moment.

'Ondine—' There was a tap at the door. 'Everything all right?'

She froze. 'Yes, everything's great. I'll see you downstairs—'

Breathing out shakily, she pulled on her clothes. She should never have let him talk her into coming back to the house, not after what had happened on the beach. It had been clear then that the danger and terror of the morning had stripped away the usual reserve between strangers.

But there was no point thinking about that now. It was done. What mattered was getting Jack out of the house and back to the hotel as soon as possible and she unlocked the door and made her way downstairs. Jack was standing in the kitchen with his back to her. He was gazing down at the counter and her footsteps faltered as she saw what he was looking at.

'What are you doing with those?'

The worktop was covered in brown envelopes and she watched in horror as he picked up two and put them to one side. 'I'm playing Go Fish.'

'Do you mind?' Pushing past him, she gathered up the envelopes.

'You have a lot of unpaid bills,' he said softly.

'And you have a lot of nerve.' Her eyes narrowed on his face. 'Look, just because we had sex doesn't give you the right to go poking around in my things—'

Yanking open the drawer, she stuffed the envelopes inside, then slammed it shut. Heart thumping against her ribs, she turned to face him. He stared at her impassively.

'Putting them in there's not going to help make them go away.'

'Well, luckily for you, how I make them go away is none of your business,' she snapped.

Jack was leaning against the counter, sunlight and shadow criss-crossing his face in tigerish stripes. 'But it could be,' he said after a moment.

She glared at him. 'I think it's time for you to leave.' Snatching up her car keys, she stepped aside to let him pass, but he didn't move. Instead, he stared at her, his golden eyes hot and bright in the tiny kitchen.

'What would you say if I told you that I could make all of those bills just disappear?'

'I would say you probably need to go back to the hospital for a CAT scan,' she said stiffly.

He smiled then—a quick, devastating, get-out-of-jail-free smile that made her breath catch.

'And on any other day I'd probably agree with you, but today is different. Today is your lucky day. You see, I have a proposition, a proposal really. I need something that I think you can provide. A service.' His eyes rested on her face, then dropped to the swell of her breasts. 'And if you were to provide that service I would be willing to recompense you. Generously recompense you.'

There was another silence. Her face felt as if it were on fire. 'Are you offering to pay me for sex?'

He stared at her. 'No, actually. As much as I enjoyed myself that wasn't part of the plan, but it could be—'

'What plan?' She cut him off. The room was starting to spin.

'I want you to marry me.'

CHAPTER THREE

ONDINE STARED AT him in silence. 'Is this your idea of a joke?' she said finally.

He frowned. 'A joke? No. I couldn't be more serious.'

'Right.' She was suddenly so furious she could barely speak. 'So you want me to believe that when you woke up earlier you suddenly realised you'd fallen in love with me and that you had to marry me?'

Behind him, there was a vase of cream roses and their lush romanticism seemed to highlight the bitterness in her voice.

'Close.' His eyes flickered over her face, then past her through the window to the distant glitter of Palm Beach. 'But what I really want is for everyone else to believe that.'

What was he talking about? Her heart gave a thump. Maybe she should take him back to the hospital.

'I don't know why you're looking so worried,' he said softly. 'It was you who gave me the idea.'

'Me?' Her heart gave another lurch.

His golden eyes rested steadily on her face. 'Marriage is good for men. That's what you said.

People think they're more dedicated, responsible, mature.'

'That's why you want to marry me? Because of some random comment I made—'

He was shaking his head. 'I don't want to marry anyone. But I do need a wife. Not for very long. A year or two at most, I haven't really nailed down the details—'

'And now there's no need to.' Stepping forward, she pushed her hands against his chest, ignoring the feel of his muscles, the way everything inside her pulled taut. 'Because it's time for you to go back to your hotel—'

It was as if she hadn't spoken. 'Look, I get it. It sounds crazy—'

'That's because it is crazy, Jack. You're crazy.' He wasn't moving and, glaring up at him, she snatched her hands away.

'It's not crazy. It's completely logical. Unconventional, maybe, but logical, and entirely practical for both of us,' he added, as if he were offering to do a car share to work. 'You need money and I need a wife.'

'Unconventional would be wearing a ball gown to go to the mall. And nobody *needs* a wife, Jack. Not in this century anyway. And I certainly don't need or want a husband. I've had two already.'

She had thought that would stop him in his

tracks, but he just lounged back against the counter, seemingly unperturbed. 'So you're an expert.'

'Obviously not. Otherwise I'd still be married.'

'Maybe you haven't met the right man.'

Her chest was pounding with disbelief. And yet she couldn't look away. 'You can't possibly think that's you.'

He studied her now for a long, level moment. 'Actually, I do.' He tilted his head, that mouth of his pulling into a mocking curl. 'We have nothing in common and neither of us have any desire to get married but—' he held up his hand as she opened her mouth to protest '—it's for exactly those reasons that in this very specific instance I think we would be right for each other.' He took a step closer, his golden eyes holding her captive. 'Think about it. No more money worries. You could be debt-free. You wouldn't have to work two jobs.'

No debts. Only one job. The possibilities filled her, stunned her. She felt his eyes on her face. He looked calm and complacent. The complacency of one who was used to winning.

She folded her arms across her chest. 'And what do you get out of it? Why do you need a wife?'

'You don't need to worry about that.'

'Then you don't need to waste any more of my time.' She had found out the hard way that other people's agendas mattered as much as her own. Not that she was planning on taking him up on his offer.

Jack stared at her for a moment, and then he shrugged. 'My grandfather is the CEO of the family business. He's also eighty-two years old. He needs a succession plan, someone to take over when he steps down. That's me.'

'Congratulations!' She glared at him. 'But I don't see what that has to do with marrying me.'

'It doesn't. Not directly.'

Catching sight of her expression, he sighed. 'Look, I'm not going to bore you with the details but, in a nutshell, I messed up at work. So now I need to show my grandfather that I've changed, that I can change. I need to show him that I can make good life choices, that I'm mature.'

She gave a small, brittle laugh. 'And you think that proposing marriage to a total stranger nails that?'

A muscle pulsed in his jaw. 'We're not strangers.'

She felt it again, that ripple of need, and her body felt suddenly tense and loose at the same time.

'It was sex, Jack. That's all.' 'That's all' made it sound perfunctory. Mundane. It had been neither of those things. It had changed everything she thought she knew about sex. Made her catch fire, and she could still feel the flames now. His gaze hovered on her face and she knew she was blushing. 'It doesn't mean we know each other.'

'Okay, fine, we don't know each other but that isn't a problem. It's the solution. We'll be like strangers on a train.'

Her whole body felt as if it were going to implode. This was insane. Why was she even having this conversation? 'Didn't they murder each other's wives?'

His face creased with impatience. 'I just meant that together we could solve the problems we can't fix on our own.'

'I'm quite capable of fixing my own problems,' she said crisply.

He jerked open the drawer. 'So why have you got so many unpaid bills?'

Because my first husband discarded me when I couldn't get pregnant and I felt ugly and stupid and useless so I married a man on the rebound. Only he liked to have fun and I couldn't face another divorce so I shut my eyes to the fact that we were spending more than we earned.

But that was nobody's business but hers.

'They're old bills. Most of them are paid off,' she lied.

'So take the money and go on a cruise. Buy a new car. If not needing the money is the biggest problem you can come up with, then I think it's a go.'

'Our biggest problem is that nobody is ever going to believe that we're madly in love.' That wasn't true either. Everybody would believe she was in love with him, but men like Jack Walcott didn't marry waitresses or lifeguards except in the movies.

'Particularly your grandfather.'

'My grandfather's a romantic and I can be very convincing.' His eyes locked with hers and she felt heat surge through her, a heat that scorched her skin and flooded her veins. 'Look, you're overthinking this. Maybe it would be easier if you just treat it as a job.'

'I have a job.'

'You have two. Both low-paid, going nowhere.' He glanced around the small, shabby kitchen. 'I can change your life, Ondine. I can change your brother's life. Think about that. If you won't do it for yourself then do it for him.'

For a moment, she saw herself through his eyes and felt a flicker of shame. So many failures in such a short time.

And then anger bubbled up inside her. How dared he stand there and judge her when everything had been handed to him on a plate? Make that a platter, she thought, catching sight of the gold signet ring.

'My brother doesn't need your money and you know nothing about my life.'

His beautiful mouth curled. 'You have two ex-husbands, you work two jobs, and you could wallpaper your house with final demands. What more is there to know?'

'Nothing. And there's nothing more to say either,' she said coldly. 'I'll call you a cab.'

He stared at her speculatively. 'You know where to find me when you change your mind. Just be discreet—'

She yanked open the door. 'You can wait on the deck. Goodbye, Jack.'

Curling up on her side, Ondine hugged her duvet closer. It was nearly an hour since Jack had left and she had another two hours before she would have to head into work. But she was going to need every minute of those two hours to get her head straight. To get Jack and his ridiculous, patronising offer out of her head.

Her heart thudded hard as she remembered the curve of his mouth and that lift of his eyebrow. He thought he knew her but he didn't know anything about her. He didn't know what she needed.

She felt something stir inside her. Okay, maybe he did, but that didn't count. It shouldn't even have happened.

Her heart leapt against her ribs as her phone

rang, and as she glanced down at the caller ID, she started to smile.

'Oli?' There was a crackling sound. 'Oli—can you hear me?'

'Yes, I can hear you.'

She could hear the excitement in his voice. 'How are you? How's it going?'

'I'm fine. And it's going really well. Yesterday I inoculated about a hundred children and today I watched a woman give birth.'

He sounded so young, so pleased with himself and she felt a rush of pride and love. 'That's amazing, Oli.'

'It really was. But we can talk about that in a minute. What's happening at home? How's Dolores and Herc? Did you get the car fixed?'

'Dolores and Herc are fine and, *no*, I haven't got around to sorting out the car yet. And everything here is the same old, same old,' she lied. 'You know...waiting tables, standing by the pool.'

Oh, and having sex with a man she'd rescued from the sea.

'I miss you—'

There was a lump in her throat. 'I miss you too. But you're enjoying it, aren't you?'

'I am.' She heard him take a breath and when he spoke again his voice was quieter, more serious. 'I didn't say anything before I left, but I was worried, O, you know, that I might come out here and realise that I'd made a mistake. Because of always being so certain. But it's everything I thought it would be, and so much—'

The crackling sound was back.

'Oli. Are you there?'

The phone clicked and she frowned as the dial tone filled her ear. This happened every single time. But he would call back—

On cue, the phone rang and she snatched it up.

'You were saying something about making a mistake,' she teased.

'Ondine?'

She almost dropped the phone. That wasn't Oliver. It was her ex-husband. 'Vince?'

'How are you?'

Her shoulders stiffened. *Poor. Stupid. Lonely. All of the above,* she thought, but instead, keeping her voice casual, she said, 'I'm good. Busy, actually.'

'Right, that's good.'

She frowned. She hadn't heard from Vince in nearly ten months. There was no need. Both of them had moved on. Which meant he was at a loose end or he wanted money.

'You know what, Vince, I'm waiting on a call so perhaps we could do this another time.' Like never.

'I wish we could, honey, but this can't wait. You see, something's come up, and we need to talk about it.' There was a silence and then Vince sighed. 'I didn't mean for it to happen. I honestly thought it would be a good investment otherwise I would never have suggested it.'

A cool shiver ran down her spine, and she felt her insides tighten. 'What are you talking about?'

'It's Oli's college fund. I'm sorry, Ondine, but it's gone. It's all gone.'

So that was that.

Breathing out unsteadily, Ondine tucked her blouse into her skirt and pushed her feet into her shoes. It had taken just over an hour for Vince to explain what had happened. Just over an hour for her brother's dreams to turn to ashes.

She couldn't just blame Vince. She might have asked him to help her invest the money but Oli was her brother. She should have looked into the fund, researched it properly, and then kept a closer eye on it, but she hadn't. Later when Vince's exuberance with money had seemed more clueless than charming, she had been relieved that the money was locked away where he couldn't get his hands on it. It had never occurred to her that the investments might tank.

There was nothing that could be done. She'd rung the college and they had been very kind but all the scholarships had been allocated. The best option, they'd said, was for him to reapply the following year, but there were no guarantees.

The lump in her throat seemed to grow a little. She needed a drink. What she didn't need was to have to go into work and face Jack. Maybe she should call in sick—

But then she thought about what she could make in tips, and right now every dime counted. Only it would never be enough. Particularly as she had other bills to pay. She thought back to how Jack had jerked open the drawer in the kitchen. No more money worries, he'd said. She could see his eyes watching her.

Feel his hot, urgent mouth against her throat.

She felt the hair on the nape of her neck rise, and then her nipples tightened.

It was indecent, the effect he had on her. And dangerous. She would be mad to spend any time in his company, much less marry him. But what other options were there? She could go to the bank. But she only had her salary. And even if she took on all the extra shifts on offer, she had less than five months to make up the difference.

Her heart felt as if it would burst through her ribs. Could she do it? Could she marry Jack Walcott?

Of course she couldn't. It was a crazy idea. He was rude and reckless—

And rich.

But also rude and reckless, plus she had failed to stay married twice before for real, so how could she possibly manage to fake it? Easy, she thought, her mouth trembling. Because Oli needed that money.

Twenty minutes later, knots forming in her belly, she was stalking through the hotel gardens to the beach bungalows. You know where to find me when you change your mind, he'd said. Arrogant bastard, she thought, but he was right. Like every other woman in the hotel, she knew exactly where Jack Walcott was staying.

Stopping in front of his door, she knocked immediately, not wanting to give herself time to change her mind. As the door opened, she felt her mouth dry. He was bare-chested, and he looked as though he had been sleeping.

'Come in.'

As she hesitated, he raised an eyebrow. 'You want to do this in the corridor.'

She didn't want to do it at all but her wishes came secondary to her need for money.

'So, how may I help?' he said softly, closing the door behind her.

'That proposal you made earlier. Is it still on the table?'

There was a short silence and, watching his

lazy cat's smile tugging at his mouth, she almost turned and walked out.

'It is.'

'Then my answer is yes. I will marry you.' Taking a breath, she steadied her nerves. 'This is how much I'll need.' She held out a piece of paper.

He looked at it, his face impassive.

'That won't be a problem.'

Silence followed, a long grainy silence that seemed to scrape against her skin. 'And I'll need some of it upfront,' she said finally. 'Shall we say half?'

The Miami-Dade courthouse was surprisingly busy for a Wednesday.

Then again, maybe it wasn't. Jack glanced at the people crossing the foyer. Maybe he was just feeling claustrophobic because today was the day.

He felt his shoulders stiffen as a door opened and a couple stepped into the hallway, hands entwined, faces lit up with happiness and relief. They might as well have had *Newlywed* stamped across their foreheads.

'Congratulations,' he murmured as they walked past. But they only had eyes for one another. Because they were in love. They believed in the power of love.

More fool them, he thought, watching them leave. He caught sight of his reflection in the mirrored lift doors. He was not, despite what people assumed, vain about his appearance. Mostly, when he looked at himself he saw the parents who had abandoned him. But it wasn't every day that a man got married.

Married.

He glanced down at the bouquet of cream roses in his hand, his heartbeat accelerating. Theoretically, he could have asked Carrie. But then it had all blown up that night on the boat and she had said that thing about his mother and after that he couldn't even look at her.

And this was better. He was calling the shots and that meant it would be easier when he wanted to extricate himself. Which he would do at the earliest possible moment. But he still couldn't shift the feeling that he was caught in a trap. Was this really his only choice?

He could have begged his grandfather to let him come back to work. Try and prove himself worthy. Only it would be harder to quantify the change because his work ethic wasn't that far removed from his grandfather's. And he was just as, maybe more, proud of the family business as John D. Walcott IV. The difference between them was that nobody knew that because he acted as if he didn't care. It was the same with school and university. With friends and partners.

But he had learned the hard way that there was

a downside to caring, and that downside was too high a price to pay.

And that was why this was his only option. Why today, just eight and a half weeks after he'd proposed to her, Ondine was going to become his wife.

Ondine Wilde: he knew her surname now, but what else did he know about her?

Truthfully, not much.

They had hardly seen one another since she had knocked on his door. Partly that was because she worked such long hours. But he also didn't want to draw attention to their 'relationship' and have it filter back to his grandfather before he was ready.

For his plan to work it needed to look as though they had married on impulse after a whirlwind romance but, as with his grandfather, that moment of recklessness would lead to a lifetime of unshakeable love and devotion.

His eyes locked with their mirror counterparts. It was going to be a tricky conversation. His grandfather might be in his ninth decade, but he was not some dithering old man. He had a fierce, enquiring mind and much as he hoped to see Jack settle down, he would want it to be with the right woman.

Jack breathed out silently. And for the kind

LOUISE FULLER

of wife he needed—temporary, emotionally detached, pragmatic—Ondine was the right fit.

He had a sudden, sharp memory of her frantic fingers, the press of her mouth, her body fusing with his, and his groin tensed painfully. She was the right fit in other ways too. But her mouth, her body were not part of this particular equation. Neither of them had specified that in the paperwork but they hadn't needed to. Sex meant intimacy and intimacy meant complications, and the point of this 'marriage' was to keep things simple.

His hands tightened around the bouquet. What had happened in her bedroom was a one-off. And yes, it had felt right in the moment but—

A pulse of heat ticked across his skin.

Actually, it had felt sublime. There had been a honeyed sweetness to her touch, hot and fierce, soft yet strong, so everything he wanted in a woman but had never found. But it didn't mean anything. Or rather it meant nothing more than the obvious, which was that there had been a bed, and they'd been alone and she was a woman, and he was a man. Nothing to see here, folks. Just hormones and hunger and—

He felt his pulse slow, and almost let the door slam in his face.

A woman was standing at the top of the staircase, and for a moment he didn't recognise her out of her various uniforms. And then he did.

Ondine was wearing an ivory-coloured jacket with a matching skirt that flared out above her ankles and some kind of veiled sunhat. Her glossy brown hair was loose and she wore no jewellery. But beneath the veil, her blue eyes gleamed like sapphires.

'Hi,' she said quietly.

He stared at her in silence, holding himself still. They had agreed to dress up for the ceremony, not too over the top. No morning suit or frothy meringues, but enough to make it feel romantic.

At the time, it had been just words. He didn't have a romantic bone in his body, as more than one of the women who had referred to themselves as his girlfriends had reminded him on more than one occasion. For him, romance, like falling in love, was a closed book, but then he'd had no experience of either. His grandparents were devoted to one another, but his grandmother died before he was born and all of his memories of his parents' marriage were of the two of them shouting and slamming doors. As for their remarriages—

A knot tightened in his stomach.

Even before the accident, it was clear there was no place for him in either of their reconfigured lives. Their houses, possessions, even their photographs had all been carefully separated and curated to edit out their shared past.

Nothing remained. Except him. He was the only reminder of the mess they'd made and that was why they kept him at arm's length.

'You made it,' he said, more for something to say than because he had doubted that fact.

She frowned. 'I said I'd be here.'

'You did.' He felt the knot in his stomach loosen. 'And you always do what you say you will.'

'Are those for me?' She gestured towards the flowers.

They had agreed to forgo all the wedding extras like a cake and confetti and flowers but on the way to the courthouse he'd spotted a florist and remembered the roses in Ondine's kitchen and on impulse he'd bought them.

'Yes.' He nodded. 'I know we said to keep things low-key, but I thought they'd help with the optics.' He held them out, and as she took them the movement caused her jacket to part a little. His pulse jerked. She had nothing underneath her jacket.

'You look beautiful.'

She gave him another of those 'whatever' kind of looks. 'You don't need to say that.'

'You're right, I don't. I said it because I wanted to, and because it's true.'

There was a sliver of silence like a crescent moon as her blue eyes met his through the veil and then she said with a studied carelessness, 'Do you have the rings?'

He nodded. Plain gold bands. He had been going to choose platinum but then he had remembered the flecks of gold in her irises when she had looked up at him. He could see the same flecks now.

'Shall we go in?'

As she nodded, he reached down and took her hand. He felt her tense and then her fingers tightened around his and they turned together and walked towards the marriage ceremony room.

Inside, the Florida sunshine was pouring in through the windows as if it really were a celebration of their joyful union instead of a pragmatic, mutually beneficial contract.

The officiant greeted them warmly. Jack shook hands with the courthouse-provided witnesses, and then the ceremony began. There were a couple of sentences about the promises they were making and the new life they were about to begin together. Thirty seconds later, they were on to the familiar 'do you, Jack, take Ondine to be your wife?' And then it was time to exchange rings.

Jack's teeth were suddenly on edge. Before it had been just words but now as he stepped forward to take Ondine's hand he felt his chest pull tight.

'I give you this ring as a symbol of my love and devotion as we join our lives together today.'

Now it was Ondine's turn. She repeated the vows carefully, lifting her face to his, her blue eyes wide beneath the veil, just as if she were his bride, but her hand shook a little and it suddenly occurred to him that she had said these vows for real and he felt a sharp stab of something almost like jealousy imagining her in the arms of other men, men she loved.

The officiant began speaking again. 'By the virtue of the authority vested in me by the State of Florida and the American Marriage Ministries, I now pronounce you married. Congratulations!' Taking a step backwards, he smiled at them. 'You may kiss!'

Ondine was looking up at him but instead of moving closer as he lifted the veil, she hesitated, and he felt the tension in his jaw spread down through his body.

Normally it was the women he hooked up with tying themselves up in knots about their predecessors, but he got the feeling that there was some unfinished business between Ondine and her ex-husbands, a sense that their shadows still loomed large in her life, and he found himself wanting to erase them from her memory so that, instead of the G-rated kiss he'd planned, he wrapped an arm around her waist and jerked her closer. Caught off balance, she fell against him, and he fitted his lips to hers, kissing her deliberately, thoroughly—

He felt her shock, and her breath, soft and warm against his mouth, and then her lips parted and she was pulling him closer, her fingers tightening in his shirt and he forgot that she wasn't his for real and the mess he had made of his life and that she shouldn't move him this way, like flames licking all over his body. He didn't think, he just was, and she was fire in his hands and his mind was nothing but heat and longing and hunger—

As suddenly as he'd started the kiss, she pulled away, cheeks flushed, breasts rising and falling with each breath. She looked as stunned as he felt. But he could guarantee that she wasn't thinking about her ex-husbands, he thought with a satisfaction he didn't understand but couldn't stop himself from feeling.

'Would you like me to take some photos?'

They both turned to where the officiant and the clerk were smiling, and, reaching into his jacket, Jack pulled out his phone and handed it to the officiant. And then turning to Ondine, he smiled too. 'That's exactly what we want, isn't it, darling?'

Leaning back against the soft, suede upholstery, Ondine pressed her hand against the armrest. At the other end of the private jet, Jack was talking to one of the stewards. He looked relaxed and calm; exactly like a man should look after marrying the woman he had fallen madly in love with.

She, on the other hand, felt as if she were falling out of the plane without a parachute. There was a kaleidoscope of butterflies in her stomach, her limbs were stiff with tension, but then she had barely slept last night. Every time she dozed off, Jack would be there beside her, *inside her*, and she would jerk awake, body quivering, pulse racing because, even though she didn't want to marry him, apparently her body was in thrall to his touch, a contradiction that was making her feel even more tense.

She shifted in her seat. In the past, she had never understood the fuss people made about sex. Before her first time with Garrett, she'd wanted to have the kind of sheet-twisting, urgent sex people had in the movies, and she'd assumed that it would be like that for her. But the first time had been awkward and uncomfortable and as the months had passed and she still hadn't been pregnant, it had become charged with a kind of desperate and unspoken blame.

As for Vince... They'd met when she'd been at her lowest point, and it had been like having a golden retriever bounce into her life. He was handsome and happy, and always excited to see her and, swept along by his adoration and enthusiasm, she'd found it was easy to ignore their complete and utter lack of chemistry in bed.

And then suddenly there was Jack who was everything she had ever wanted in a lover but who lacked everything she needed in a man. Only now he was her husband.

No wonder she wasn't sleeping.

The cause of her insomnia was nodding at something the steward was saying and rubbing the back of his neck in a way that made her feel hot and irritable and on edge.

Ever since she'd agreed to marry Jack, she had been desperately ignoring the real-time consequences of that decision. Mostly it had been easy enough. Work had been full-on and she'd even taken on extra shifts. Now, though, she was on her honeymoon and there was nothing to distract her from her thoughts.

She shivered on the inside. Except Jack.

He shouldn't have kissed her like that. As if they were alone. As if it were real. And she shouldn't have kissed him back. But then again maybe it was the jolt she needed to make her wake up and smell the coffee.

She felt her stomach twist. *No, not coffee.* She was running on adrenaline as it was, she didn't need to add caffeine into the mix.

But she did need to wise up. There would be no more kissing except the closed-mouth variety. And they absolutely would not be having sex again. She would not allow one heated encounter to cloud the issue. Marrying Jack was about moving on, moving forward past this mess she'd made so that Oliver would have the future he deserved, the future her parents had planned for. Not making an even bigger, messier mess of everything.

As Jack said, this was just a job, and like all her jobs she would do it to the best of her ability. So she would play the adoring, lovestruck wife in public and keep things cordial but cool behind closed doors.

'Darling, I'm sorry that took so long.' She looked up, and her heart lurched as Jack sat down beside her. 'Did you miss me?'

Glancing at the stewards, she pasted a smile on her face. 'Of course.'

He stretched out his long legs. 'Apparently, it's forty-six degrees on Whydah. Honestly, we might as well have gone to Banff.'

They were en route to Martha's Vineyard where they would pick up a launch to his family's private island off the coast of Massachusetts.

Jack had wanted to fly to the Caribbean but then she had pointed out to him that she was supposed to have reined him in. 'I thought you wanted to show your grandfather you could change, that you were changing,' she'd said to him at one of their brief covert meetings. 'That means not having a splashy honeymoon and drinking champagne for breakfast.'

Not that the air stewards knew that, she thought a moment later, hearing the pop of a cork. 'Thank you,' she murmured as the chief steward appeared, beaming, a foaming glass in each hand.

Lifting the glass to her lips, she took a sip, and frowned. Great—now her adrenaline was making the champagne taste weird. Maybe she would just go and brush her teeth.

'I might just go and freshen up,' she murmured to Jack. 'I'll be back in a minute.'

Astonishingly there was a bedroom on board and an ensuite bathroom. If only she could stay here for ever, or at least the rest of the flight, she thought, leaning forward to rinse out her mouth.

But it wouldn't change anything. She glanced down at the plain gold band on her finger. They were married. And Jack had already spoken to his grandfather.

She had chickened out of telling Oli. But that was different. He was so far away, and alone. And besides, she was still trying to come to terms with what she had done. She let out her breath slowly, trying to steady herself. It was just a lot. Not just getting married, but this jet. The private island. *Jack.* Her pulse accelerated and she was back at the kiss at the courthouse again. There was definitely going to have to be some rules.

As she walked back into the bedroom, her stomach flipped and more annoyingly she felt her nipples tighten. Jack was stretched out on the bed, his sprawling limbs complementing the lazy-cat smile on his face.

'What is it?' she said, somewhat ungraciously she had to admit, but she felt oddly panicky at being suddenly and completely alone with him.

'What do you think it is?' His beautiful mouth curved down into a frown. 'You're my wife. We're supposed to be madly in love. So why are you skulking in the cabin like some stowaway?'

'I'm not skulking. I just needed a bit of space.'

'Since when?' Shifting against the pillow, he tipped back his head. 'You didn't seem to need any at the courthouse.'

Ignoring the treacherous warmth spreading through her limbs, she said coolly, 'You seem to be confusing your needs with mine.'

He gave a short laugh.

'So when you were pulling me closer, that was you trying to do what, exactly? Pick fluff off my jacket?' He sucked in a breath. 'Just admit it. You wanted to kiss me as much as I wanted to kiss you.'

'What if I did?' She was too shocked by his admission to be anything but honest with him. 'That doesn't make it right, and you know it. Yet you still acted on it.'

Dropping onto the bed, she kicked off her shoes. 'And that there is your problem, Jack. That lack of understanding and childish disregard for anything but what you feel in the moment is why you've ended up marrying a complete stranger to get your life back on track. Because presumably your grandfather, and everyone who has the misfortune to spend time in your company, has had enough of you.'

His face was harsh like stone. 'I cannot believe I thought we could make this charade work.'

'The feeling's mutual,' she snapped.

CHAPTER FOUR

JACK STARED DOWN at the magazine he was holding, a frown creasing his face. He liked this writer, and usually he found her accessible and informative, but she must have changed her style because he couldn't remember a word of what he'd just read.

But then he hadn't actually been reading the article, just pretending to.

His lip curled. It was bad enough having to fake things in front of Sally and the rest of the staff at Red Knots. But to be doing so on his own time, when they were alone—

He glanced over at the cause of his current inability to focus. Ondine was also reading. A book. Only, judging by the tiny vertical indentations on the smooth skin of her forehead, she was, unlike him, completely engrossed in the contents. Her mid-brown hair hung loose today, as it had most days since they'd reached the island. He liked it that way. Liked the way it shone too in the afternoon sunlight that was filtering through the window.

At that moment, she lifted her hand to tuck a stray strand of that same hair behind her ear and her cuff fell away from her wrist. Remembering what that delicate nub of bone felt like beneath his fingers, he felt his skin begin to prickle.

Oh, for—

Gritting his teeth, he swore silently as the rest of his body caught up with the scene replaying inside his head, and he felt his groin tighten. If this were a normal marriage, a normal honeymoon, he wouldn't be sitting here on this sofa pretending to read magazines, he would be in bed with his wife. Or maybe he would still be sitting here, but Ondine would not be wearing clothes and her hand would be touching him, not her hair.

But there was nothing normal about their situation.

Not that he had any idea of what 'normal' was when it came to married life. Before he'd started kindergarten, his parents' marriage was already stumbling towards the lawyer's office and a *decree nisi*. As for their remarriages. His visits were too brief, too rushed and too infrequent for him to get any insight into how their relationships worked.

Of course, his grandparents had a gold-standard marriage. But all that remained of their blissfully happy union was photos of the two of them at various stages of their lives and his grandpa's unwavering devotion to her memory.

Imagining John Walcott's reaction to finding

out the truth about his grandson's marriage, Jack shifted uncomfortably in his seat.

He and Ondine had agreed to tell their families about the wedding after the ceremony, and he had called his grandfather outside the courthouse. Thinking back to that conversation now, he felt his pulse stutter. It was difficult to surprise an eighty-two-year-old man, but he had managed to surprise his grandfather.

'Married?'

'I know what you're thinking, Grandpa.' His voice had felt raw in his throat. 'And I know why you're thinking it. I've not been any kind of grandson, not the sort you deserve—'

'Jack, that's not true—'

The softness in his grandfather's voice had almost made him unravel with guilt.

'Please, just let me finish. I know I've let you down, but I do want to change, and I think I am changing, and Ondine…she's part of that change. Right from the start, it felt different with her. I feel different when I'm with her. And I know you understand that. I know you felt that with Grandma—'

His chest had tightened. His grandfather had met his future wife when she was working as a waitress. Nobody had supported the match but love had prevailed. It had felt wrong to bring up his grandmother but it had worked.

'I did. I still do,' his grandfather had said softly. 'I was so unhappy when we met. I'd inherited the business and I had all these people relying on me, only I was too proud to admit I couldn't cope. Too ashamed to admit that I hated the burden.'

Jack had frowned. He hadn't known that. 'I thought you loved the business.'

'I grew to love it. But back then, I was miserable. Then I met Candace, and it's no exaggeration to say that she saved me. She "saw" me, the real me. I found myself telling her things I'd never told anyone else. I suppose you could say I shared my soul. That's when I realised I loved her. You see, that's what love is, Jack, sharing your soul.'

'I think that's probably long enough, isn't it?'

Ondine's crisp question cut across his thoughts and he turned towards her, an anger that was both irrational and unfair skimming across the skin. Because he had wanted this cool, transactional relationship. Except now that he was living it, he didn't like it at all.

Although to say that he'd wanted this was giving him slightly too much credit. True to form, he hadn't got much further than the wedding ceremony in his head, and as a consequence he hadn't worked out how to do this part of the marriage.

Night-time was easiest. Having already told Sally that upstairs was off-limits to her housekeeping team, they slept apart, in adjacent rooms, and each morning he let himself back into what was supposedly the room they shared.

Days were harder.

They had established a routine of sorts. At some point in the morning, then again after lunch, they would retire upstairs and sit in silence at opposite ends of the bedroom. Then, after a decent amount of time had passed, he would go back downstairs, looking suitably rumpled, and say that Mrs Walcott was sleeping and anyone who happened to be there would smile and nod in silent but tacit understanding.

And on that first day it had seemed to work. But now, pretending to be exhausted from some daily honeymoon sex marathon while simultaneously enduring a period of self-imposed celibacy was pushing his buttons almost as much as these absurdly stiff and overpolite conversations.

Maybe it would have worked if they hadn't had sex. But being in such close proximity to her made him feel as if he were drowning again and the only thing he wanted to hold on to and be held by was Ondine.

'Absolutely,' he said, glancing at his watch. 'It's the penultimate day of our honeymoon so I think we could justifiably be a little worn out today.'

He had chosen his words with care, wanting to provoke a reaction, and as her chin jerked up he saw a bright flare of temper snap in her eyes like lightning across a stormy sky. But her voice was cool as she said, 'I'll be down in about an hour.'

He watched her for a moment, his breath scratching his throat.

'Take as long as you like,' he said finally, and, cutting himself off from her narrowed blue gaze, he strode across the room, wishing he could as easily excise his body's reaction to that flush of colour winging across her cheekbones.

Desire. A yearning to reach out and touch. And irritation at what she was feeling. He saw all of it. Felt all of it because he was feeling it too.

It had been like that since the flight to Martha's Vineyard. After their spat, Ondine had sat on the bed, toed off her shoe, curled up on her side and fallen asleep. Of course, having followed her in with a stupid grin on his face, he could hardly have emerged moments later looking like a puppy with his tail between his legs so he'd had to sit there, fuming, with not even his phone to keep him occupied until she'd woken up just as the plane had started its descent.

Only what was there to fight about? It wasn't as if theirs was even a real marriage.

He pictured the stubborn curve of her spine, and his mouth twisted. He shouldn't be that surprised. Everyone turned their back on him in the end. Even someone who was being paid to be his wife.

He knew why she was snippy. It was that kiss at the courthouse. But they were supposed to be crazy in love; and at some point in the not too distant future they would have to do all those things that couples in love were supposed to do, and it would need to look 'real'.

Besides, it had been their wedding day—he could hardly just have given her a peck on the cheek. And *she* had kissed *him* back.

What he really wanted to do was remind her of that fact. He clenched his hands. *Liar.* What he wanted to do was stalk back into their bedroom, snatch that book from her hands and then kiss her until she shook with need.

In reality, what he was going to do was take her to Martha's Vineyard. His jaw clenched. He hated shopping. Normally wild horses couldn't drag him near a mall. But after three endless weeks of being in forced, fruitless proximity with Ondine he would willingly wander around every upmarket boutique on the island if it meant not having to spend another hour pretending to read a magazine while trying to ignore yet another inappropriate daydream about his so-called wife.

Martha's Vineyard was every bit as charming as Ondine had expected and the total opposite of glitzy, over-the-top Palm Beach. Here, everything was quiet, low-rise, slow-paced. The one thing it shared with Palm Beach was that it was clearly a magnet for the wealthy and famous.

Just a different kind of wealth and fame, she thought, sidestepping a woman with a toddler to get a better view of a former US president, his wife and their security detail as they crossed the street and disappeared into a bookstore.

'Is that—?'

'Yes.' Beside her, Jack nodded. 'I would introduce you, but I want to keep a low profile until you've met Grandpa.'

'You know him?' She couldn't keep the surprise out of her voice, and, glancing over, she saw the pride glittering in his golden gaze.

'He's a friend of the family.' His hand, which had been holding hers loosely, tightened so that her wedding band pinched her finger. 'That's the gallery I told you about. Shall we cross over?'

It was a rhetorical question. He was already stepping off the sidewalk.

Should she have married him?

That was not a rhetorical question so much as an irrelevant one. They were married, but had it been the right thing to do? Here, now, walking in the sunshine, it felt as though it was. But only because she was pretending she was on holiday, not on her honeymoon.

Her *fake* honeymoon.

She thought back to the strange routine that had

somehow evolved without either of them saying a word. In theory those hours in the bedroom at Red Knots, when she and Jack were supposedly making love, should be the easiest. Nobody was watching so they didn't have to play their parts. They should have been able to relax, but she had never felt more tense, not even during the last gasp of her previous two marriages.

And she knew that was absurd, only that didn't stop it being true.

Remembering the feel of his flickering, golden eyes as he glanced across the bedroom, a shiver moved through her and with it a tactile memory of warm skin and his mouth hard on hers. But obviously, the honeymoon was always going to be the hardest part. After this, they wouldn't have to spend nearly as much time together, so maybe she should follow the example of the ex-president and his wife, and enjoy this downtime.

It wasn't just politicians enjoying the lack of traffic lights and chainstore-free vibe of Edgartown. She recognised two actresses, one chat-show host and a comedian from one of those late-night Saturday shows. But there were no paparazzi, no passers-by filming them on their phones. Everybody just went about their business, popping in and out of the white-painted boutiques, farm shops and cafés.

Her pulse danced forward. And yet, even

dressed casually with his features disguised by a baseball cap and sunglasses, Jack, being Jack, somehow still managed to draw admiring looks from the women walking past. It wasn't just his looks. There was something about Jack Walcott that made you look twice.

And then it was almost impossible to look away.

As if to prove her point, a pretty young woman with blonde hair and a floaty white dress who could have given Helen of Troy a run for her money glanced over, her cheeks turning a fetching shade of palest pink.

She felt a jolt of jealousy, as sharp as it was irrational. Jack was her husband, but in name only. Most of the time she wasn't even sure she liked him. They had no relationship. No shared history. Unless by history you meant one heated sexual encounter and one kiss too many.

Her skin felt suddenly too tight. She could almost excuse herself for what had happened on that first day. They had been in shock, both of them unravelling with the enormity of what could have happened. But that kiss at the courthouse had been cool-headed, unscrupulous on his part, anyway. And she was angry with him. For not knowing, or, if he did know, not caring about the effect it had had. Glancing over her shoulder, she caught the young woman staring after her enviously. But then maybe it happened so frequently, he'd stopped noticing.

If only she could do the same.

The gallery was as cool and quiet as the clientele milling in front of the paintings. She felt like a fraud. What did she know about art? Leaning in to examine what looked like a scribble of orange over a smudge of green, she noticed the price.

How much?

'Do you like it?'

She turned. Jack stood behind her, his gaze not on the painting but on her face, his eyes narrowed as if she were a puzzle he was trying to complete.

'It's interesting,' she said cautiously.

He laughed. Several people turned around and she felt her cheeks grow warm. 'Spoken like a true art critic.'

She shrugged. 'I don't understand art.'

His mesmerising gold eyes travelled over her face. 'I disagree.' He took a step closer so that they were only inches apart and the curve of his jaw and the flawless skin over his cheekbones was more fascinating than any painting and she wanted to lean in closer. To touch. To explore. To understand him.

'You know if you like something or if you don't. If you find it compelling. Cryptic. Beautiful.' The light in his eyes sharpened, and she felt her skin grow hotter and tighter.

'If you see it. If you feel it here—' he reached out and touched her heart lightly with his fingers '—then you know all you can ever know. All you need to know. You have to trust yourself.'

Her hands twitched, then bunched into fists as if she couldn't control them. 'I don't trust easily.'

'I don't either.' He held her gaze. Maybe he was holding her breath too because her head was starting to spin and she felt suddenly fragile, adrift—

Her need for him, for it to be real, banged through her like a gong, and she felt almost queasy with panic, and, taking a step backwards, she said, 'I wish I'd come here before.' She fought to keep her voice light and careless. 'Then I wouldn't have had to marry you. I could have just bought some paints and knocked up some "art". I would have cleared my debts in no time.'

Jack stared at her in silence, his teeth on edge, his body tense.

Just for a moment there, he had forgotten all of it. The mess he'd made at work. The water pulling him under. The spat on the plane and the tension of those hours spent barricaded in their bedroom.

Everything, everyone had been forgotten as her eyes had met his and the need in her eyes had shuddered all the way through him in a way that had made him feel undone.

Only then the shutters had come down and he felt like a fool, a stupid child again.

He needed a coffee. Actually, he needed a whisky, but a coffee would have to do. Catching hold of Ondine's elbow, he began to nudge her towards the gallery's café.

'I might just grab an espresso. Would you like something, darling?'

He felt her tense, and then her eyes widened and she tugged her arm free. 'Excuse me. I just…'

Now what? He stared after her, pulse ticcing with disbelief even as his brain followed the sway of her hips into the restroom.

'Would you like me to go and check on her?'

What?

He turned to the woman who had spoken. She was standing next to a man wearing a baby sling. The baby was facing outwards, fingers crammed into her mouth, her eyes the same startling blue as Ondine's.

The woman smiled sympathetically, then turned to the man standing beside her and said, 'I was just the same, wasn't I?' Glancing over at the coffee shop, she shuddered. 'Even just thinking about coffee used to set me off. But it's worth it.' Her face softened as the baby reached up, mouth opening to reveal two tiny white teeth. 'And it's actually a good sign.'

Jack stared at the baby. He was having to re-member to breathe. 'Good sign?' he said slowly.

'My doctor always said morning sickness was a sign of a strong pregnancy.' She hesitated. 'Are you sure you don't want me to go check on her?'

'No, thank you. I'll go—'

Walking away from the couple, he felt almost drunk with shock and denial. Whatever that woman was saying was wrong. How could she be right? She knew nothing. She knew nothing about Ondine or him. She was just some random—

He stopped. Ondine was walking out of the restroom. She looked pale and shaken, but her shoulders stiffened as she saw him.

'This way,' he said curtly, grabbing her hand and towing her towards the exit.

'What is it?' He felt her fingers flex against his but he didn't loosen his grip until he had pro-pelled her outside. He glanced up the street and, moments later, their car pulled up to the kerb.

'What is it?' Rubbing her hand, she turned to face him as the car started to move, her blue eyes narrowing on his face. 'What's so urgent that you have to pull my arm out of its socket?'

'I need to ask you something.' He swallowed. His heart was suddenly racing. 'Are you preg-nant?'

She stared at him, her eyes widening with

shock and confusion. 'What kind of a question is that?'

'The kind that needs answering.' His eyes locked onto hers. 'So I'm going to ask it again: is there any chance whatsoever that you could be pregnant?'

No. Absolutely not. No.

Gazing across the bathroom, Ondine felt her heart beating unevenly. That was what she had said to Jack when he had asked her if she could be pregnant, and she had believed it. She still believed it now. But the test in her hand told a different story.

Her eyes fixed on the plastic wand.

She had been here before, could picture the bathroom in the house she'd shared with Garrett, feel the swoop of disappointment as she'd stared down at the larger blank square.

They had tried for nearly two years. She had, anyway. At some point, without telling her, Garrett had given up. Suddenly conscious that her arms were shaking, she wrapped them around her waist, hugging herself tightly.

After she'd replied to his question Jack had stared at her assessingly, and then directed the driver to a side street. He had jumped out of the car, returning almost immediately without a word of explanation, and then they had been bumping

in the boat across the Vineyard Sound back to
Whydah Island and Red Knots.

Her throat had tightened. She had been so focused on trying not to throw up she had barely
registered the huge gabled house with its shin-
gled roof.

Not that Jack had given her any chance to do
so. Holding her hand with a grip that had verged
on the painful, he had more or less hauled her
upstairs through the bedroom and into the bathroom. Reaching into his jacket, he had pulled out
a paper bag and tossed it onto the vanity unit.

'Let me know when you're done,' he'd said,
and the authority in his voice had reminded her
suddenly and alarmingly that, while he might act
like a playboy, he had been raised to issue orders
and expect them to be followed. 'I'll be next door.'

She stared down at the two thin blue lines,
and then back at the instructions leaflet. Not that
she needed to read it again. When she'd been
trying for a baby with Garrett she'd lost count
of the number of pregnancy tests she had taken.
She knew exactly how they worked, and they all
worked on the same principle.

The only difference with this one was that it
was positive.

Positive.

As in pregnant. As in having a baby.

Her fingers bit into the handle of the plastic

wand. Only that wasn't possible. There must be some mistake. Only the kind of wand used by witches and wizards could conjure up the magic required for this test to be correct.

Her eyes locked onto the two lines. The first told her the test was working properly. The other told her that she was pregnant. Very slowly, she laid her hand across her stomach, her fingers flexing. But it must be faulty.

Holding her breath, she opened another box.

Then another.

And another.

Ten minutes later she was staring down at the fourth positive test when there was a knock at the door.

'Ondine—'

It was Jack. Her heart seemed to swell up and fill her throat so that breathing was suddenly almost impossible. 'Just a minute,' she said hoarsely.

'No, not another minute.' His voice was taut. 'You've been in there fifteen already.'

'All right. All right.'

From somewhere inside, she felt a snap of anger and defiance. This wasn't just happening to him. It was happening to her too.

Getting up, she unlocked the door and opened it. Jack was standing there; his handsome face was unreadable, but his eyes were bright and hard, and when they fixed on her face she felt like a deer caught in headlights.

'Well?'

It wasn't fair. She had waited for this moment for so long, hoped and prayed for it, and now it was here. But for it to happen now, with this man who didn't love her and never would, in this relationship that was a sham, a mutually convenient charade, was just too much. It was impossible to say the words out loud and instead she held out the test. He stared down at it in silence. His expression didn't change, but his breathing did.

'It's wrong,' she said quickly.

There was a tense, electric moment, and then his mouth shifted into a question mark. 'How is it wrong? There are two lines. The two lines mean you're pregnant.'

No, she thought again, swaying forward then back again. There must be some other explanation, and that would become plain. She just needed a moment to think clearly and rationally, only her head was spinning so fast that her thoughts were impossible to catch.

'I know that's what it's supposed to mean. But it's wrong. It must be faulty.' She was babbling now and he was looking at her, incredulous, stunned.

'And what about those ones?' He stalked across the bathroom to where she'd left the other tests next to the basin. 'Are these wrong too?' he said, picking them up and brandishing them at her.

'Yes. They are. They must be. I can't be pregnant.'

For a moment he didn't speak, and then, 'And yet you are,' he said slowly.

And yet she was.

Only how could it have happened? Given the odds of everything in that moment. Her history; the time of the month; the fact that Jack had worn a condom. There must be some mistake—

'You're damn right it's a mistake—'

Her chin jerked up, and, meeting Jack's angry gold gaze, she realised that she had spoken out loud. And then, registering his words, suddenly she was angry too. 'That's not what I said. I just meant that it shouldn't have happened.'

Not just shouldn't. She had thought it couldn't.

But the test in her hand said different. Her anger vanished as quickly as it had flared up and she stared down at the plastic wand dazedly, lost in the long line of failed attempts, the months of waiting, of trying not to get her hopes up. 'I don't know how it did, it's like a miracle—'

The silence that followed that remark was like a heavy, smothering blanket so that suddenly it was a struggle not just to talk but to breathe. Jack was staring at her, his powerful shoulders taut against his jacket. And then a shadow passed over his face.

'You're good,' he said softly, but there was a suggestion of contempt and menace in his voice as if he might bare his teeth at any moment.

'You really are very good.'

She stared at him in confusion. Good at what? A smile that was not a smile was curving the corners of his mouth and the fluttering queasiness she'd felt at the airport was back. Unthinkingly, she pressed her hand against her stomach and his eyes narrowed in on the movement, the not-smile vanishing from his face.

'It's impressive.'

Except he didn't sound impressed. She watched his lip curl. Or look it either.

'All of it,' he continued. 'The trembling voice. The wide-eyed shock.' He held her gaze. 'You must have had a lot of practice. Is that why you have two ex-husbands? Did you pull this sort of stunt with them too?'

Stunt.

The air snapped taut between them. Ondine blinked. A swirling misery was rising up inside her like water in a storm drain. She couldn't breathe, couldn't speak. For a moment she thought back to all the months of shame and despair and feeling a failure on so many levels. But then the hard gleam in his eyes pulled her back, and, lifting her chin, she met his gaze. 'You don't know anything about me or my ex-husbands. As for "stunts", I'm not the one jumping off boats for kicks when I'm loaded.'

'No, you get your kicks by taking someone's life and burning it to the ground. I cannot believe you thought I'd swallow this garbage.' He tossed the tests into the sink, the frustration and fury in his face rolling through her like wildfire. 'So when did you really find out? That you're pregnant, I mean.'

Her head jerked up, her gaze locking with his. 'I found out just now. The same time as you did.'

Jack leaned back against the vanity unit and again she got that suggestion of barely controlled menace. 'You expect me to believe that. I may be stupid—as I married you that's pretty much a given—but I'm not a total fool.'

Her heart gave a kick in her throat as he pushed away from the sink and took a step towards her. 'So, this is your MO, is it?'

She blinked. 'My MO?'

'Is that how you got the last two idiots to marry you?' he persisted. 'By pretending you were having their baby? Only this time you messed up. You actually got pregnant. So whose is it?' His glittering eyes tore into her. 'The baby. Who's the father?'

Shock was reverberating through her like a

train hitting the buffers. Who did he think was the father?

'You are,' she said. 'You know you are.'

He straightened then: six feet three of furious, restrained male in clothes that probably cost more than her car. 'I don't know anything of the sort. I know we had sex once. I also know that I wore a condom—'

'Maybe you didn't put it on the right way.'

'The right way?' The disbelief in his voice was partnered by an expression of pure incredulity. 'I'm not some clueless teenager, Ondine. I know how to put on a condom so why don't you stop with all the games and—?'

'You think getting pregnant is a game?' She felt her stomach lurch, and she was suddenly close to tears.

His eyes gleamed dark gold beneath the recessed lights. 'No, no, no, this is not how this goes. You don't get to be affronted, Ondine. You're not the one who's being played here.'

'You haven't been played,' she snapped, focusing her panic and anger on him. 'I'm as shocked as you are.' More so, in fact.

He was shaking his head, fury and frustration imprinted in the flawless symmetry of his face. 'I don't believe you. I think you found out you were pregnant that day I came back to yours.'

'That's not true.' The intensity of his dark gold

gaze made her feel light-headed. 'I didn't know I was pregnant until five minutes ago, and you are the baby's father and that's the truth.'

'No, the truth is that when I suggested you marry me, you threw me out of your house. But then, lo and behold, two hours later you turn up at the bungalow, all jittery and wide-eyed, and everything's changed and now you do want to marry me.' He laughed derisively. 'And you expect me to believe that it has nothing to do with this. That it was just some random coincidence.'

'It was,' she protested. And not just a coincidence. Finding out that Oli's fund was gone, and, worse, that she had been a passive bystander to its mismanagement, had been an enormous stomach-churning shock.

'So what happened in those two hours? Why did you change your mind?'

Her chest felt as if it were being crushed in a vice and she opened her eyes wide so that they wouldn't fill with tears. Listening to her brother talk about his day at the hospital, hearing the happiness in his voice, she had felt not just love but awe. He was such a remarkable person, and he would be a remarkable doctor. How could she have told him that he couldn't go to medical school? Not this year, maybe not ever if he couldn't get a bursary.

She might have messed up her own life, but she wasn't about to wreck his too—

Only telling Jack about the college fund would mean revealing so much more about herself and her life than she was willing to share with anyone, but particularly this man who already thought so little of her. She might not have money or power, but she still had some pride.

And, frankly, he wasn't in the mood to listen to her anyway. As far as he was concerned, she was guilty.

'You put me on the spot. And it was a lot to think about. I needed time to process it.' That was all true, but it wasn't why she had changed her mind and she knew it. Worse, Jack knew it too. She could tell by the curl of his lip.

His breath hissed through his teeth. 'Time to process it?' There was a harshness to his voice that made a shiver wash over her skin, and she could practically see the interrobang hanging in the air between them. 'You must think I was born yesterday.'

She stared at him, her breath hot and sharp in her throat. Years ago, she had dreamed of watching that second line appear, faint at first, then strong and indisputable. She had imagined the moment of revelation and mutual joy, and now it had happened, finally, miraculously, only there was no joy, just anger and suspicion and doubt and resentment.

'Actually, oddly enough, I'm not thinking about anything but this baby.'

His perfect mouth twisted. 'Don't give me that. The only person you're thinking about is you. You got yourself knocked up, but your baby daddy doesn't want to know, does he? Did he see you for the devious, opportunistic little hustler you are? Is that why you set this whole pantomime of a marriage in motion? Or was he just not as rich as I am?'

The injustice of his words knocked the breath from her lungs, and it was almost impossible to stop herself from reacting, to restrain herself from picking up the pregnancy tests and hurling them in his beautiful, scorn-filled face.

'How dare you?' Her hands curled into fists. 'First off, this stupid marriage was your idea. And just to be clear, you might be paying me to be your wife but that's exactly why you're the last man on this planet I'd choose to impregnate me. Do you really think I'd want some arrogant, entitled trustafarian brat like you to father my child? Because I don't,' she said, answering her own question.

'And secondly, it doesn't matter whether you believe me or not, Jack. There is no "he". There is no other man in my life—'

'Do not try and tell me this baby is mine.' He was backing away from her, the dangerous, dark undertone back in his voice. 'This is on you. It's not my responsibility—'

It.

That hurt, appallingly. Not just that he didn't believe her but that he was rejecting his baby, her baby, their baby and a bud of defiance blossomed inside her as her hands moved protectively over her still-flat stomach.

'I never said it was. In fact, I don't want it to be. I don't want anything to do with you. I want out of this stupid, farcical marriage.' Not that there was much to get out of. She had signed an NDA and a prenup and Jack had given her an upfront payment, which she would return if it meant waitressing every night for the rest of her life. But neither of them had wanted to put the sordid transactional details of their arrangement in writing.

His beautiful face creased into something angular and ugly. 'You took the words right out of my mouth.'

He spun round and stalked out of the bathroom.

Ondine stared at the space where he had been standing, anger surging through her as hot and ungovernable as the hunger that had briefly flared between them and she stormed after him but he was already at the bottom of the stairs and then he disappeared from view.

Her head was spinning as if she were drunk, and then she felt wave after wave of nausea and she turned and stumbled back into the bathroom and threw up.

CHAPTER FIVE

WRENCHING OPEN THE French windows, Jack strode purposefully across the lawn. Or that was what someone watching him might have thought. In reality he felt like a drunk man doing a field sobriety test, and the truth was he had no idea where he was going or what he was going to do when he got there.

All he knew was that he couldn't spend another second in that bathroom with Ondine and her lies and duplicity.

And that was another reason to hate her, he thought savagely, glancing back at the house.

The Walcott family owned several properties. But Red Knots was different from all the rest. Since he could remember, he'd spent part of every summer there and, for him, it was a place of simple, unthinking calm. A refuge from the uncomfortable truths of the past and the failings in the present.

It held a special place in his grandfather's heart too. John Walcott had met his wife, Candace, in Martha's Vineyard. Like Ondine, she was working as a waitress. The difference was that for John and Candace it was love at first sight. And they were still in love, holding hands and gazing into one another's eyes like loved-up teenagers in every single photo he'd ever seen of them. Right up until when his grandmother died the year before he was born.

He hadn't told Ondine that. He hadn't wanted her to get the wrong idea. To imagine that their relationship might one day blossom into something more substantial, more permanent.

But now that had happened anyway, right under his straight, patrician nose. Thanks to Ondine's duplicity, what had started out as a quid pro quo transaction was now a Gordian knot of nightmarish outcomes.

He breathed out shakily. His body was still ringing with the shock of what she had just told him. She was lying to him, of course. She must be lying. He had used a condom, *hell*, he always used a condom. It couldn't be his baby.

But what if it was?

He felt his chest tighten as Ondine's voice echoed inside his head.

'You're the last man on this planet I'd choose to impregnate me. Do you really think I'd want some arrogant, entitled trustafarian brat like you to father my child? Because I don't.'

A spasm of pressure he chose not to identify squeezed his heart.

How he lived, how he *needed* to live, was not compatible with parenthood. It wasn't even compatible with long-term relationships. That was why he'd ended up in this ridiculous sham marriage in the first place. A marriage that was supposed to be a solution to his problems, not an additional problem to solve. A marriage he had impulsively entered into knowing only half the facts.

The sound of waves broke into his thoughts and he realised that he had made his way to the jetty. Beside it, the launch bobbed jauntily on the water, her smooth fibreglass hull bumping gently against the wood in time to his heartbeat.

He shoved his hands into his pockets. He hadn't been near the sea since that morning all those weeks ago and, looking at it, he felt his body tense. Ondine had pulled him from that same water, breathed air into his lungs. She had saved his life.

Now, though, she seemed more intent on derailing it.

His mouth thinned. It wasn't fair. He had taken precautions. So, why was this happening to him?

His shoulders tensed against the warm breeze because he knew why. He had taken too much at face value. Focused on the big picture rather than examining the details. He had looked at Ondine and seen an opportunity. A woman who needed money. And because he had money to spare he'd thought that put him in charge.

He'd thought the same about that deal with the Canadians. The one that had ended with an expensive settlement and his removal from the board. Apparently, he hadn't learned his lesson.

Gritting his teeth, he glanced up at the serene blue sky. Was that what this was? Was all of this the balancing of some vast cosmic quadratic equation of which he was just a component? It certainly felt like it. He felt insignificant, wound up, powerless.

Just like when he was a child being ferried back and forth between his parents' homes. Grudgingly welcomed then passed back with almost tangible relief as if he were a low-ranking card in Chase the Ace.

His hands balled in his pockets.

And then inevitably it had happened. In their speed to get back to their new Jack-free lives, there had been a screw-up, a misstep in communications. He had broken his arm.

Sometimes he wondered about how things might have played out afterwards. If his mother hadn't extended her holiday in St Barts. Or his father had decided to wait for her to arrive, choosing to spend a few more minutes in the company of his only son instead of leaving him in the care of the housekeeper as usual.

His throat clenched and for a moment he couldn't seem to make the deck beneath his feet stay still, and, reaching out, he gripped the railing to steady himself. Of course, neither of those things had happened and that was when his grandfather had stepped in and taken him to live in New York.

But this 'situation' with Ondine was different. Whichever way he worked through this particular equation the outcome was going to be the same.

It didn't matter if he was the father of this baby or not. He had already told his grandfather that he and Ondine were married. So, if he backed out now on his honeymoon, he was going to look more flaky, less mature, less everything he needed to be to win back John D. Walcott IV's trust and respect, and his place back on the board.

For that to happen, he needed time to prove himself worthy at work. That was why he had agreed with Ondine to stay married for at least a year. By then he would have shown his grandfather that he was capable of stepping into his shoes. Then they could gradually and quietly start to live separate lives. Or that was the plan.

If you could even call it that. He ran his hand over his face, feeling suddenly exhausted.

Everything he'd assumed would happen wasn't going to work now because in a year's time, Ondine would have given birth, and the optics of leaving your wife with a small baby were about as bad as it could get.

In other words, he was cornered. There was going to be no release from this trap he had set and sprung himself, or at least not within the timescale he'd planned. And not without tearing off a limb, metaphorically speaking. Although Ondine probably wouldn't be averse to doing that in real life, he thought, picturing her small, furious face.

His mouth twisted. She had no right to be angry. He was the one who'd had his life turned upside down and inside out. But he wasn't a kid any more. He was in control. He made the decisions now, and he was deciding to make this sham of a marriage work.

He stopped breathing.

Although he might have said the opposite to Ondine.

Replaying the words they had flung at one another as he'd stormed out of the bathroom, he felt a flicker of unease. But she hadn't meant what she said. She wouldn't act on it, would she?

The waves slapping against the side of the launch seemed to grow louder, taking on the rhythm of his suddenly racing heart, and, swearing under his breath, he turned and began to walk swiftly back towards the house.

Red Knots looked as it always did. And, as always, gazing up at it quietened his mind. There was no way Ondine would make good on her threat. Even if she hadn't signed any paperwork, she needed money. Even more so now. But as he made his way upstairs, he felt another flicker of unease. The bedroom was empty. The bathroom too, and it was tidy. He stared for a moment at the vanity unit, remembering how he had tossed the pregnancy tests into the sink. Then he turned and checked the other bedrooms and bathrooms.

But there was no sign of her.

Downstairs, heart accelerating, he moved from room to room. In the kitchen, the housekeeper, Sally, was weighing out some flour. Aside from that, the room was empty and he was beginning to panic.

She couldn't have left the island. There was only one boat and that was tied up at the jetty. So short of swimming back to Martha's Vineyard—

Surely she wouldn't attempt that. But then he remembered how she had pulled him through the water, and the steadiness of her grip around his chest. Only that had been close to shore. Here the currents were swift and treacherous. Slamming back outside, he made his way around the veranda, feeling sick to his stomach—

He stopped short.

Ondine was sitting on the porch swing, hugging her knees to her chest. She was wearing the same clothes as earlier but her feet were bare now. It made her look more delicate, more vulnerable, younger than before. Like a child playing dress-up. And in a way that was what she was. What this was. Except they couldn't just change out of their clothes and go back to being who they were. Not yet anyway.

'I thought you might be swimming back to the mainland.' It was harder than it should have been to keep his voice calm.

Her blue eyes met his. She looked pale and tired, but defiant. 'I agreed to be your wife. If I say I'm going to do something, I do it.'

Even as his anger simmered inside him, he felt a twitch of respect, admiration even. And relief. 'You did say that,' he agreed. 'But you also said you wanted out of this farcical marriage.'

There was a short silence.

'You said you wanted that too,' she said finally. He watched as she let go of her knees, stretching out her legs. Her feet seemed suddenly particularly bare, so bare that he was distracted by their soft curving arches and then, with crashing predictability, by a memory of how the rest of her body looked naked.

He gritted his teeth. He needed no reminder.

'I did. I do. Only I think we both know that can't happen. So, it looks like I'm stuck with you.'

He didn't bother hiding the bitterness in his voice, but as she hugged her knees closer to her chest he wished he had. Then he told himself that he didn't care. That it was her fault for trying to trick him into taking responsibility for another man's mistake.

Her chin tilted up. 'And I with you.'

She made it sound as if the idea appalled her as much as it did him and it shouldn't have stung as it did. But her words scraped against old wounds inside him. 'As if! You wanted this, all of this.'

'You're wrong,' she said flatly. 'I wanted to pay my bills. That's all. That's why I agreed to marry you. And I know you don't believe me, just like you don't believe that you're the father of this baby, but both those things are true.'

Now she got to her feet. 'I can't prove the first so I'm not going to try to.'

She was standing close enough to him that he could have counted her freckles. Close enough that he could smell the clean, floral scent of her hair. Close enough that if he wanted to, he could have reached out and pressed her body against his.

'But I can take a paternity test,' she said quietly.

His heart thumped against his ribs. If she was offering to do that she must be pretty sure he was the father. He felt an ache in his stomach, like hunger, except he had no appetite. He was the son nobody wanted. His parents had next to no input in his life. How could he possibly raise a child?

What the hell are you talking about?

He swore silently. Of course he wasn't the father. He'd get better odds on there being a white Christmas in Palm Beach. They'd had sex once. He'd worn a condom.

And condoms were only ninety-eight per cent effective.

He felt panic jump in his throat. But why? The odds of a condom failing on that one occasion were minuscule, and besides it was all too much of a coincidence her 'finding out' she was pregnant after they were married.

It was just the nearness of her throwing him into a state of confusion, making his head swim, and he hated that she could do that to him, and it was easier to hate her. Neater. Less unsettling. In fact, it was a relief.

'Do one, don't do one.' He shrugged. 'It's your call. But don't think for one moment that it's going to change anything because it won't.'

The skin over her cheeks looked taut, and her mouth was trembling a little but when she spoke her voice was steady. 'You're right, it won't.'

Staring down at her, he frowned. He'd thought she'd protest, argue, throw her offer back in his face but she was calm and her face was still and shuttered.

'Don't worry, Jack. I'll say what you want me to say. I'll hold your hand and look into your eyes and smile at you for as long as it takes to convince your grandfather that you're the man he wants you to be. The man you can never be in reality. And then we'll go our separate ways like we agreed. And as for this baby.'

She took a step backwards, just as she had that day in the bedroom when all of this had been set in motion. 'You were right about that. This baby is never going to be your responsibility so as of now that topic of conversation is off-limits.'

'That won't be a problem,' he snarled.

'I didn't imagine it wou—' She broke off, her face tensing.

He frowned. 'What is it?'

'I'm going to be sick,' she said hoarsely and, eyes widening with panic, she clamped her hand to her mouth.

It was some three days now since Ondine had told Jack that he was not responsible for either her or her baby. Those words were in his head when he woke up every morning. They stayed with him as he fell asleep.

He frowned. And yet here he was, still on Whydah, watching her sleep. Shifting forward in his chair, he stared down at her, his eyes resting on her still, pale face.

But he still wasn't convinced that he should be there. In fact, most of the time he felt like an imposter.

His frown deepened. Because he was one. Their marriage might be legal, but legal was different from real. And the reality was that he was paying Ondine to be his wife; only he needed facts to fit the fiction and, ironically, the only fact that would stand up to robust scrutiny was a pregnancy that had nothing to do with him.

His hand tensed against the armrest as Ondine moaned in her sleep.

Except it did. Whether they discussed it or not, this baby was making its presence felt, twenty-four-seven, because, despite its name, the sickness didn't just happen in the morning. If anything, the nausea was worse at night. Which was why she was sleeping now, at two o'clock in the afternoon, leaving him to play the doting husband sitting by her bed.

For the optics, obviously. He could hardly abandon his wife in her hour of need. But also, because he couldn't seem to look away from the woman he had called a devious, opportunistic little hustler. All of which was still true. But in light of everything else that was happening right now, it just seemed to matter less.

The doctor had repeated what that woman had said to him at the gallery. That the sickness was typically the sign of a healthy pregnancy, and he understood the science of it. But looking over at

Ondine's pale face, he still found it difficult to believe.

About as difficult as it was to believe that he was the father of this baby.

His shoulders stiffened. They hadn't talked about that particular ticking time bomb since that day out on the veranda. But then they hadn't talked much at all. Mostly because Ondine was either in the bathroom being sick or sleeping like now. If they happened to be in the same space she spoke, not to him, but in his general direction. Those occasional snatched conversations they'd had were brief and joylessly polite.

'You can go. I can manage on my own, thank you.'

She'd said that on the first day when she had unlocked the bathroom door and found him waiting for her in the bedroom. Wearing plain grey sweatpants, some kind of stretchy top and with her dark hair twisted into a kind of low, messy bun, she could have been heading off to some yoga class. Only the dark smudges beneath her ridiculously fluttery eyelashes gave any indication of the exhausting days and disrupted nights.

'You don't need to do this,' she told him after another moment as if she'd needed a breath or two to regroup before she could speak again. 'You don't have to stay. Just go and catch lobsters or whatever it is you normally do when you come here—'

'When I normally come here I'm not on my honeymoon.'

Titling back her face, her eyes met his. 'Well, I'm sorry if you're disappointed, Jack, but if you're hanging around hoping that—'

That stung. Did she really think so poorly of him? His jaw tightened. 'Seriously, don't flatter yourself. Once was enough.'

'Then you won't mind leaving,' she said coldly. 'We were only hiding out together so we could pretend we were having sex but we're obviously not doing that now.'

Her face had tensed then, just as it had out on the veranda, and she'd bolted back into the bathroom.

But she'd said exactly the same thing each time she returned to the bedroom, her mouth flattening when she saw him, and he knew he should be relieved. But for some reason her stubbornness had infuriated him, and so yesterday afternoon when she'd repeated the exact same words, he'd shaken his head and said, 'That's not going to happen.'

'Why not?' she countered immediately.

Her face had no colour at all. Even the blue of her eyes looked washed out, like faded denim, and he could hear the exhaustion in her voice. He knew that she was struggling. But she had already thrown one spectacular wrench into the works, from now on they were going to do things his way.

'Because it would look odd. What would Sally think if I just left you being sick on your own?' With Ondine being so ill, he'd had no choice but to tell the housekeeper and the rest of the staff. But he'd also made it clear the pregnancy was too early to be announced. That at least was something he could control.

She'd shrugged. 'I'm sure you'll think of some suitable explanation, Jack. You can be very convincing, remember?' Beneath the fatigue there was a jaggedness that set his teeth on edge.

'And I'm your husband, remember?'

'No, you're the man I married for money.'

That was inarguable but he still felt as though he'd been kicked by a horse. 'That still makes me your husband.'

There was a hard pause, and then she gave a small shake of her head. 'Only on paper. It isn't real.'

'But your morning sickness is.' His eyes locked with hers. 'That's why I'm staying.' During the hours of daylight anyway.

A faint tremor ran through her body. She lifted her head and stared at him mutely, her face set into taut, wary lines, and for a few half-seconds he was tempted to reach out and smooth them

away with his fingers. Fortunately, before he
could act on that impulse, she turned and, heart
beating out of time, he watched her walk away,
and he kept watching right up until she closed the
bathroom door behind her.

CHAPTER SIX

AT FIRST HE thought someone was laughing. That she was laughing.

It was a quarter to midnight. He was sitting on his bed, his eyes fixed on the connecting door to Ondine's room.

It was the room his grandfather had set aside for his parents to use when they visited Red Knots. But despite having a nanny in tow, neither his mother or father had considered it relaxing to vacation with their young son, so it had been his grandfather who took him to the island, his grandfather who comforted him when he had a nightmare or a stomach ache that stopped him from sleeping.

Now he wasn't sleeping for a different reason.

There was a faint strip of light under the door but that wasn't what had caught his attention. It was the noise, faint, intermittent, jerky, fading to silence, then swelling again—

Crying, not laughing.

Shoulders tensing, he glanced away to the window. Outside everything was black on black and so quiet. Not a creature was stirring, not even a mouse. Just his conscience, he thought with a flicker of irritation as he found himself staring at the door again.

But why? Ondine wasn't his responsibility. Their marriage wasn't real. She'd said so herself.

'But your morning sickness is.' He gritted his teeth. That was what *he'd* said so that he could override her wishes.

Had she known that? He didn't know. But it appeared that he wasn't quite enough of an arrogant, entitled trustafarian brat to just sit here and let her struggle with her nausea alone.

Whether or not there was anyone there to see it.

He got to his feet. This was a mistake on so many levels—

Ondine was sitting on the bathroom floor, her face resting on her elbows, her elbows resting on the side of the bath, her back rising and falling jerkily. Her shoulder blades looked like angel's wings. Gazing down at her, he felt his ribs tightening. Now what?

'Ondine?'

At the sound of his voice, she froze, body stiffening, but she didn't look up at him. Instead, stifling a sob, she turned her head away so that he couldn't see her face, her arm curving protectively around her stomach.

'Are you okay?' He winced inside. Stupid question. She clearly wasn't. 'Can I get you anything?' Better, but not much.

She was shaking her head, not meeting his eyes. 'No, I... Could you just go?' She made a harsh little sound as if her throat were too tight. 'Please. I don't want you here.'

A muscle ticced in his jaw. Okay, job done. He had asked, and she had answered, so he had done more than most men would in his situation, but for some reason his legs didn't seem to want to move.

He gritted his teeth. 'But I can't leave you. Not like this.'

She was sick then. At first, he just stood there, feeling helpless and superfluous, but the second time it happened, he crouched down and caught hold of her hair, bunching the silky strands into a loose ball. Her neck was hot and damp but she was shivering as if she was cold, and he felt a stab of anger for the man who had let her deal with this alone.

Except she wasn't alone. He was there, he realised with a jolt.

'It's okay, you're going to be okay.' He kept talking quietly, calmly, the words forming with an ease that surprised him. It seemed unlikely that she was even listening, but then at one point she looked up at him, her face pale and tearstained.

'You don't have to do this—be here.'

The shame in her voice scraped against his skin and he had a flashback, vivid as a photograph,

of coughing up seawater onto the sand and Ondine gripping his shoulder, the pulse in her hand
steadying the choking panic in his chest.

'You're right, I don't. I'm choosing to be here.'
Heart banging, he sat down beside her. 'And the
only reason I'm here to make that choice is because of you.' She looked up at him and the soft
blue of her gaze tugged at something inside him.
'Because you saved my life.'

She was only sick one more time after that. He
sat on the edge of the bath while she washed her
face and brushed her teeth and then followed her
back into the bedroom.

'I'll be fine now.' Her voice was husky and the
smudges under her eyes looked darker, but her
face was no longer pinched with panic.

'Okay. But if you need anything, I'm just next
door—' He cleared his throat. 'But you know
that—'

She nodded, lifting her head slightly so that
she was looking at a point just past his shoulder.
'I'll be fine. I just need to get some sleep. We
both should.'

We.

The word pinged inside his head, tripping the
automatic alarm that was his early warning de-
fence system against any kind of intimacy and
obligation.

It was one of the many exhausting contradictions of his life. He hated being alone, but he couldn't let people get close either. To do that would mean trusting them to stick around when he messed up, and he didn't trust easily.

We was a signal to cool things down. *We* meant that he needed to take a step back. *We* conjured up a lifetime of hastily exited hotel suites, arguments and half-hearted promises that made his body brace and his weight shift to the balls of his feet like a sprinter getting ready to run.

His heart skipped a beat.

And yet he didn't feel like running now, any more than he had in the bathroom when she was being sick. On the contrary, he felt as if there were some kind of forcefield pushing the two of them together.

Of course, that was probably because, as co-conspirators in this sham marriage, he and Ondine were already a 'we' of sorts. What other reason could there be? They had no history. No trust. This baby was her future, not his. What else was there between them?

Sex.

The hair on his arms rose stiffly and he glanced over to where Ondine stood watching him in an oversized grey T-shirt he hadn't even registered before, his whole body tensing as that blunt, un-prompted answer was accompanied by a crys-talline memory of her lips parting as she rocked against him. Above the sound of his heart, he could hear those noises she'd made in her throat of half need, half abandonment as he'd driven into her.

Was she remembering it too?

Or was she remembering when he'd told her that once was enough?

His hands curled at his sides and he was on the verge of telling her that he hadn't meant what he'd said and that he regretted saying it, but then he came to his senses. 'I'll say goodnight, then.'

She nodded, and he was already backing away from her when she spoke.

'Goodnight. And thank you…' She hesitated as he looked over at her and he could see her pulse jerking in her throat. 'Thank you for staying with me. It was kind of you.'

She was thanking him? His chin jerked up and as his eyes met hers, he saw a confusion that matched his own as if she couldn't quite believe what she had just said.

He shrugged. 'I'm glad I could be of some help.' And strangely, he was.

For a moment, they stared at one another in silence separated by a few feet of Persian carpet and then he said quickly, 'I'll see you tomorrow.'

Except it was already tomorrow, he thought, as he finally got back into bed. Outside the darkness

was fading away. Now everything looked grey.
The colour of compromise.

The C-word.

His mouth twisted. Compromise was not normally part of his vocabulary. Or his life. And this
marriage wasn't supposed to be any different. In
his head it all seemed very black and white. His
money in exchange for Ondine's collusion. Marriage as a performance.

But earlier when he had gone to find her in the
bathroom, he had chosen to carry on in character
even though there had been no staff around and
it had been just the two of them. And while he'd
been holding her hair and stroking her back, everything had loosened into something less rigid.
More grey. No longer just in or out, but somewhere in between.

And he could live with that.

In fact, it had been a little naive to assume there
wouldn't be some overlap, some kind of compromise. He rolled onto his side, his eyes closing.
But that didn't mean he was about to get caught
up in her lies.

Now that was progress.

Gazing down at her empty plate, Ondine sank
back against the cushions. She had finished two
whole slices of toast and, instead of nauseous,

she felt light-headed, intoxicated almost. Was that possible? Could you get drunk on food?

It didn't seem likely, but the last few weeks had taught her that anything was possible, no matter how unlikely. Miracles did happen, and, frankly, she was just relieved to not be feeling sick.

For almost all her life she had taken her body for granted. Unlike, say, her ability to recall facts or make good decisions, it was the one thing she could rely on and most of her life she had done so unreservedly. And then on that day trip to Martha's Vineyard everything had changed. Each morning she woke up feeling as if she were a stranger, living in the same body but utterly changed. Since then, she had been forced to adapt on an almost hour-by-hour basis.

As of now, water and flat Gatorade were in; coffee was out. She still couldn't even think about dairy produce and watching a film where the two lead protagonists ate pizza had made her skin turn clammy. But she was definitely feeling better and, thanks to Sally, she was starting to tentatively enjoy eating again.

The housekeeper really had been incredibly kind.

And she wasn't the only one.

Pulse stumbling, Ondine glanced across the table.

She and Jack were having breakfast outside on

the deck and anyone looking at them would think they were the perfect honeymooning couple. And Jack, louche in plaid pyjamas and a white T-shirt that emphasised his muscle-defined chest and arms, with his handsome face tilted up to the warm mid-morning sun, looked like the perfect husband.

He had been acting like one too.

Or maybe she didn't mean acting, because that was what he did when other people were around—like now. And that was simply a box-ticking exercise designed to corroborate their marriage.

What she was talking about was how he behaved when it was just the two of them alone.

Picking up her glass, she took a sip of water. That first night, when he'd come into the bathroom, she had wanted to crawl into a ball and hide beneath a carapace of impenetrable spines. It had been bad enough being sick but to have Jack there watching—

She had thought he would leave her to it. After all, he couldn't have made it clearer that he wasn't responsible for this baby.

Her hands moved instinctively over her stomach as she remembered her own shock and disbelief and fluttery astonishment when she'd gazed down at the positive tests. After so long trying for a baby, to discover that she was pregnant with a

man who was paying her to be his wife had been
too much to take in. It hadn't felt real, but then
almost immediately she had started being sick
and all her doubts had been confounded, forgotten. Irrelevant.

Jack's too, maybe, she thought, her gaze ar-
rowing in on his beautiful profile. Was that why
he sat with her every night? Her sole guardian in
those hours when the world shrank to the walls
of their ensuite bathroom? Scooping back her
hair. Talking nonsense to her in that beautiful,
easy drawl of his while she retched and shook
and wept.

She felt her heart thud hard inside her chest.
He hadn't said as much. But what other reason
could there be?

'What's up?'

Looking up, she felt her pulse stumble. Jack
was frowning across the table. Unlike most people when they frowned, his features didn't grow
harsh. Instead, it made him appear more as if he
had been cast in bronze.

Glancing away, she wondered how long would
it take to get used to his beauty? A lot longer than
their marriage would last, she thought with a distant sort of jolt.

'Are you feeling sick again?'

He was leaning forward now, looking concerned, and she knew he was only doing so be-

cause Sally was nearby, but she couldn't stop herself from wondering what it would be like if he weren't just playing a part but really cared about her.

She shook her head. 'No, I was just thinking that I've never seen such a perfect lawn.'

As his dark gold eyes moved past her shoulder to the rectangle of flawless green grass, she took a steadying breath. She might not be throwing up any more, but she was definitely suffering from sleep deprivation because there was no way Jack Walcott would ever see her as anything but a means to get his life back on track.

And she didn't want him to. Didn't want him. *Liar.*

Her cheeks felt suddenly as if they were under a heat lamp. Okay, that might be something of an exaggeration. The truth was that whenever she let her mind wander, she could think of nothing but those feverish moments in her bedroom and how his lips had tasted and the way his hands had made her forget everything but the need pounding through her body.

But was it so surprising that memory had imprinted in her head? So much had happened that day, so many big emotions unleashed, a connection formed beneath the water, her breath moving through his body—

'You need to tell my grandfather that when you

meet him.' Jack was looking at her now, his eyes glittering in the sunlight. 'The croquet lawn is his pride and joy. We could play a game if you like.'

She laughed. Because it was funny. Not that long ago she had been serving drinks to this man. Now he was her husband and he was inviting her to play croquet with him.

'Why are you laughing?'

'It's just the idea of me playing croquet. That's not who I am.'

He smiled then, a curling, devastating smile that seemed to slide over her skin like sunlight and turn the sun into just another distant, indistinguishable star and she thought, not for the first time, that it had been a lot easier in some ways when they'd had the buffer of their hate between them.

'Maybe you don't know who you are,' he said softly.

She stared at him, his words pinballing inside her head, the slow burn of his gaze making her breath catch. It was a shock to hear him say out loud what she had been thinking for so long. But the truth was Jack was right. She didn't know who she was. Had never really known even when she was growing up.

But then, it was more about what she wasn't than who she was. Her mum, her dad and Oli were all so clever, whereas she had struggled at school to be anything but average. For a short time, she had been above average at swimming, but a shoulder injury had forced her to pull out of training. A week later she'd met her first husband.

Garrett had been handsome, hard-working and impatient to begin the life he'd had mapped out. And she had been at the centre of that life. Until she couldn't get pregnant and then in the space of a few months she'd become a divorcee, an orphan and a surrogate parent to her teenage brother.

Devastated, terrified, adrift, she had stumbled into her second marriage and out the other side into her subsequent divorce. Poorer but no wiser, apparently, she thought, gazing across the table at her third husband. And even just thinking that made her cheeks hot and her skin prickle.

She had married Jack for Oli's sake, but what did that make her? A sacrifice? A fool?

And what about after it ended? Who would she be then?

Glancing up, she realised Sally was waiting to clear away the plates.

'I did think about maybe wandering down to the beach,' she said quickly, wanting, needing to change the subject and drag the path of her thoughts onto a firmer, less unsettling footing. 'I feel like I haven't left the house for weeks.'

You could see the ocean from every window, and it was pleasant sitting here in the sunshine surrounded by the artfully arranged shrubs and trees, but now she was feeling more herself, she craved the raw, untouched beauty of nature.

There was a brief blink-and-you'll-miss-it silence and then he shrugged, his smile still in place. 'Sure, why not?'

It took six, maybe seven minutes to reach the curving beach. As they walked over the top of the shallow dunes, Ondine felt like a pilgrim stepping off the *Mayflower*.

She had wanted raw and untouched, and this was it.

Pristine, powder-fine, bone-white sand, speckled at the shoreline with pale pebbles, stretched in either direction. In the shelter of the bluff, the bleached remains of a tree lay on its side like a fallen statue. Beyond the sand, the Atlantic rippled like molten glass.

It was absurdly beautiful, spectacular, dramatic, and it seemed astonishing to her that it all belonged to just one family.

All except the sea. That didn't belong to anyone.

'It's amazing,' she said quietly.

Jack nodded, the warm breeze stirring his fringe as he toed the sand with his shoe. 'I think so.'

Shielding her eyes from the mid-morning sun, she let her gaze drift over the mesmerically shifting waves. The sea was different here...not blue like in Florida. In fact, it looked almost lavender-coloured.

'It's hard to believe that's the same ocean as back in Palm Beach. That we could have swum in that water.' As she spoke, what looked like a fishing boat chugged into view and she had a sudden, vivid flashback of Jack leaping into the air—

Beside her, she felt rather than saw him tense and she bit the inside of her mouth, wishing she could bite back her words. Was he seeing it too? Was he feeling the sudden shock of impact? The downward drag of the water, relentless, inexorable, his limbs weakening as the oxygen spilled from his lips.

'Have you gone back in? Into the sea?' She hesitated. 'Since it happened, I mean.'

There was no need to specify what 'it' was, but Jack frowned almost as if he didn't understand and then he shook his head. 'Not yet. I haven't had time.'

Hadn't he? That seemed unlikely. Unlike her, he wasn't working at the moment, and, aside from some fairly undemanding paperwork, the wedding had been a work of moments to arrange.

'You have time now. Maybe we should go for a swim after lunch.' Glancing over at the shifting water, she saw it again. His body beneath the waves, the glint of his signet ring.

'Or we could just go for a dip in the pool.' There were two. One was outside, shielded from the ocean breezes by fat laurel hedges, the other was indoors. With steps leading into the water, either would be the perfect place to regain your confidence. 'It doesn't have to be a big deal, it's just I think the longer you leave it before you get back in the water, the worse it will become. It's like falling off a horse. You need to—'

Up until that point, he'd kept silent, now though he cut across her. 'I know the theory. In fact, I've fallen off plenty of horses, so you don't need to labour the point.'

'I wasn't,' she protested. 'I just thought it might help if—'

'I don't need your help. More importantly, I don't want it, so, if you're done with your amateur sports psychology—'

His face was blank of expression but the hostility in his voice shocked her into speaking.

'I'm not an amateur. I'm a trained lifeguard and a qualified swim instructor and, as it happens, I was on the national junior swim team for two years and we worked alongside sports psychologists all the time.' She took a breath. 'Look, I know what happened was shocking and horrible but, trust me—'

'Trust you?' He stared at her in silence, a stillness forming around his beautiful golden eyes, and then she almost jumped out of her skin as he laughed, a short, biting laugh that echoed around the empty beach.

'You think I trust you? That I could ever trust you?' He was shaking his head. 'Then you're not just devious and opportunistic, you're deluded.'

Her chest felt as if it were bound in barbed wire. She stared at him, shocked, stung by the abrupt renewal of hostilities between them. She had thought they had moved on. That something had changed and softened between them, but now she saw that she had done what she always did: read motives into actions and then turned them into a better story than the one she was living.

'I was just trying to be nice. That's all, Jack. But I don't know why I bothered because you're really not worth it.'

She was suddenly, brutally tired of him and of the two of them and the wrongness of everything and, without waiting for him to reply, she spun away and began to walk back towards the dunes.

He was unbearable. Unreasonable. Unkind. Her heart pounded in time to her footsteps across the sand, then faltered. He was also the father of this baby. Later, she would wonder if that thought made her look over her shoulder, but in the moment, all she registered was the blank-page emptiness of the beach.

Jack was gone.

She had turned and, before her brain had time to catch up with the impulse of her body, was moving across the sand and then her footsteps faltered.

He was sitting on the fallen tree, his eyes fixed on the sand, his shoulders hunched in a way that pinched at something inside her. He looked like he had that day in Oliver's bedroom when finally the shock of the day had risen like a wave and pulled him under.

And now he was drowning again.

He didn't look up as she stopped in front of him, but for some reason that made her more determined to stay. 'I know how hard it is for you to trust me because I feel the same way about you,' she said quietly. 'But I do want to help you.' If you'll let me, she wanted to add.

He flicked her a glance as if he'd heard her unspoken words. 'You wouldn't understand.'

'Try me.'

His face was taut, and she knew that whatever it was, he couldn't say it out loud. But then his stillness and silence reached inside her, pushing everything out except one tiny incontestable fact and she realised that she already knew. That, deep down, she had always known.

'You can't swim,' she said quietly.

He didn't reply but again he didn't need to. She

could feel the truth in the sudden escalation of tension in the air around them.

How could that be possible? But sadly, she knew that it was not just possible but statistically unremarkable. Around half the population of the US could either not swim at all or not well enough to save themselves, although Jack was wealthier than the statistical average.

She looked over to where he sat, staring straight ahead without expression. But he didn't need her to tell him that.

'How far did you get in learning?'

Silence, then, 'Not far.'

'Does anyone know?'

His face was shuttered. 'No. It never came up.' A pause and she could feel him reaching for a plausible explanation. 'My parents split up when I was young. It was quite messy.' Another pause. 'I had two sets of nannies, and I went to a lot of different schools. I think it just got missed off the to-do list. And later on, it seemed too late to do anything about it.'

Out at sea, the fishing boat was just a tiny bobbing dot. Watching it, she replayed the moment when she had looked out to sea and seen Jack run across the deck and leap.

The memory winded her. 'But you jumped off the yacht.'

A muscle flickered in his jaw. 'I know.' There

was a note to his voice she couldn't place and as if he'd heard it too, he got to his feet. 'I didn't plan to. And I wasn't drunk or high. It was a stupid impulse thing. I was tired and I'd had enough of everyone and I wanted to get off the yacht, and I was looking at the water and it suddenly seemed ridiculous that I couldn't swim. I mean, how hard could it be?'

Now he looked winded.

As the silence stretched away from them she held herself still. He was staring down at his hands, hiding his eyes, she thought, but then she saw that they were trembling.

'Not hard. If you know what you're doing.' She kept her voice matter-of-fact. 'And it's even easier if you're not wearing clothes.' She hesitated, then took hold of his hands. 'Everyone is a beginner at some point, Jack. You'd learn in a heartbeat. You just need someone to teach you. And I can do that. If you'll let me.' She said the words out loud this time.

She watched him, waiting, on edge suddenly at how badly she wanted him to trust her. At the shoreline, the waves seemed to hover mid-air, their white caps quivering. As they toppled over, Jack shifted his gaze and when he looked back, his beauty took her breath away all over again.

'Okay.' He nodded, his mouth curving up at the corners, and in the past she would have got lost somewhere between that crooked smile and the beating of her heart, but she knew now that some of his smiles, this one, for example, were designed to distract, to divert attention away from what was going on inside that beautiful, sculptured head.

'You can teach me to swim. On one condition. You let me teach you how to play croquet.'

The lightness was back in his voice now so that it was hard to tell if he was being serious, but she decided to play along. 'Deal!'

Picturing the flawless, rectangular green lawn, she added, 'Although I'm not sure where croquet is going to fit into my life.'

His gold eyes locked with hers. 'But this is your life. Our life,' he added, after a moment.

It was just words, she told herself, but suddenly her heart was thumping inside her throat and all she could think about was his hands on her body, and the clench of her muscles around his hardness.

They were standing a breath apart, his hands still entwined with hers, and they stayed like that for what felt like a long time, not moving, not speaking, just staring at one another as the air around them shifted, and tightened, pressing against them, pushing them closer—

'We should probably be getting back,' he said, dropping her hands and taking a step backwards.

'Otherwise Sally will think something's happened and we don't want her sending out a rescue party.'

It wouldn't make any difference if she did, Ondine thought, panic beating like a gong inside her chest as they headed back to the house in silence, because the only thing she needed rescuing from was herself, and her body's senseless yearning for the man walking beside her.

CHAPTER SEVEN

'COME ON, JACK. Don't phone it in. Keep pushing, keep pushing. There you go—and rest.'

Breathing out heavily, Jack lowered the hex bar to the floor of the gym and released his grip on the hot metal. His skin was coated in sweat and it felt as if every muscle in his body was screaming abuse at him. Splaying out his fingers, he let his head fall back against the wall, his eyes narrowing on his personal trainer's impassive face.

At home, Mark was a family man, the father of twin girls and a devoted husband. In the gym he was a soft-spoken but relentless taskmaster.

As if to remind him of that fact, Mark said quietly, 'Thirty seconds left. Use the time. Stay focused.'

They worked for another ninety minutes. After strength training they did mobility drills, followed by a session with the punchbag, finishing off with a cool-down and then finally it was over.

'Good workout.' Mark smiled. 'But maybe do some yoga later. You were losing focus a little,' he added by way of explanation as Jack gave him a narrow-eyed look. 'I know you're not a big fan but building muscle and increasing endurance can only happen with the right mindset.'

They shook hands. 'See you on Wednesday.'

Jack nodded. 'Wouldn't miss it.'

'You can try,' Mark called over his shoulder. 'But you know I'll find you.'

Picking up his protein shake, Jack took a gulp. Mark was based in New York, but they had trained in London, Paris, St Barts, Tulum, Ibiza. They weren't friends. Truthfully, he knew as much about his trainer now as he did when they started working together four years ago and yet, after his grandfather, Mark was probably the most constant, most reliable person in his life.

Jack glanced around the silent gym. His heartbeat was still elevated from the training session but there was another beat behind it, not of panic, not yet, but he could feel it creeping in from the edges, just as it always did whenever he was alone and there was nothing to distract his thoughts from slipping into the dangerous territory of his past.

Not just his past, he thought, his chest tightening.

From the outside, it looked as though he were part of a series of overlapping social circles. There were friends of the family, friends of friends, people he knew from the various schools he'd attended and all of them were regular fixtures at the parties and events that punctuated his calendar.

But were they his friends? Could he trust them? Did they care about him?

He stared across the gym, his breath jabbing his throat as if it were a punchbag, the panic lost in the numbness that was pushing into the gaps between his ribs.

Is there anyone I can call?

Ondine had asked him that all those weeks ago when the shock of nearly drowning had finally caught up with him. Her question had been simple enough, and it came, he knew, from a place of concern. But the answer he hadn't given, the answer he was too ashamed to give her was, no: there was no one. Not his so-called friends, none of whom had bothered to check up on him that day. Not that it was all their fault. He'd been hurt too early, too much, too often to allow friendship to happen. Speaking of which—

His muscles were burning, and his hands throbbed from hitting the punchbag but as he tried imagining his parents' reactions he felt an older ache in his chest.

He knew exactly how it would have played out. If by some miracle his mother had picked up, she would no doubt have told him to call his father. But what would be the point? His stepmother always fielded his calls and she would probably just have said what she always did, which was that his father would call back.

Fat chance.

He knew from experience that if he had waited for that to happen he would still be sitting in the hospital now.

There was only one person he could have reached out to: his grandfather.

And he'd wanted to call him so badly that day in Palm Beach. But he had called him so many times in the past. There was the DUI in LA; the party in that hotel in Cannes when the room got wrecked; the arrest in Aspen for possession of a controlled substance. All of them managed and tidied away quietly and discreetly by a man who had been a guardian, a mentor, a father as much as a grandfather. John Walcott was the one person who cared about him, and enough to dispense tough love.

And he had wanted to prove he was getting his head straight, recalibrating his life, only what had happened on the yacht hardly qualified for either. But that wasn't the only reason he hadn't dialled the number. He'd known that if he heard his grandpa's quiet, authoritative voice he would weep.

His jaw clenched. He hadn't cried since he was five years old and he fell off a chair and broke his arm. He could remember the sharp snap as his elbow hit the floor, the bright white pain that blurred his sight.

Later, at the hospital the nurses kept telling him he was brave, but he wasn't. It was just that he knew then there was no point in crying; that the power of tears to stop bad things from happening only worked in fairy tales.

None of which changed the fact that his grandfather had cared and worried about him for three decades already. For once, he hadn't wanted to add to those worries.

Besides, he was scared that if he started weeping he might never stop.

Outside the window he caught a flicker of blue the exact colour of Ondine's eyes and, glancing down at the swimming pool, he felt his heart miss a beat. That wasn't what had happened with her. Okay, he hadn't actually wept but he'd been closer to tears than he'd ever been with anyone.

He could see her fingers as they curved around his, feel their warmth and the firmness of her grip. It was the same steady grip she must have used when she'd pulled him from the sea. He had only the briefest memory of it before he'd lost consciousness but in that shifting liminal space between water and air, life and death, the touch of her hand had been reassuringly, unquestionably real.

And it had felt just as real yesterday afternoon.

When Ondine had asked whether he had been swimming since the 'accident' he had panicked and done what he always did. He'd pushed back, and, as expected, she'd stormed off. *But*—and this was a first—she had come back and he had ended up telling her the truth.

Not every sordid detail but it still felt seismic. *To her too.*

He could see, *feel* her shock and confusion, but she hadn't given up on him like his parents or chosen to look the other way like his so-called friends. Instead she'd taken his hand and sat with him just as she had at the hospital and afterwards, while he'd slept in her brother's bed.

A brother she clearly adored. And yet, she was also a manipulative little hustler who had tried to convince him that he was the father of her baby.

Only how could she be both?

He felt his body tense. It was a perplexing question but now that his savage anger at being caught up in her pregnancy had subsided and he was spending more time with her, it was one he wanted and needed to answer.

Who was Ondine Walcott? At various times he had cast her as opportunistic, devious, manipulative and yet he had seen no evidence of any of those qualities. Instead she was bright and funny, intermittently furious and, on occasion, downright infuriating. But she was also patient, compassionate, a good listener. And sometimes, when she didn't know she was being watched, he could sense a shadowy fatigue that had nothing to do with the pregnancy.

Only if he had been wrong about who Ondine was, then could he be wrong about other things too? Could this baby be his? He felt a twinge of panic in his chest. Someone as damaged and incomplete as he was had no business fathering a child. He wouldn't know where to start.

But Ondine would, and maybe she could teach him.

He thought back to how she had offered to teach him to swim. *If you'll let me,* she'd added.

Would he let her? He stared down at the pool, his heart bumping against his ribs, remembering the moment out on the bluff when there had been other, more urgent things he'd wanted to let her do. Other things he'd wanted to surrender to. And not just surrender to. He had wanted to seize with both his hands—

His groin tightened, a shiver moving through him and over his skin as his body relived those heated, frantic moments in her bedroom when his mouth was hard on Ondine's and he was hard inside her, harder than he'd ever been.

He couldn't forget it; he'd wanted to. Especially after she'd told him about the baby. And he assumed he would forget as he always did, although sometimes forgetting merged with pretending it had never happened. Either way, afterwards, he'd been certain that it was just a kind of PTSD, a feverish, lost-in-the-moment compulsion to hold onto something, to someone that had been feverishly and swiftly satisfied.

A pulse of heat beat across his skin as he pictured Ondine's upturned face out on the beach.

Except he didn't feel satisfied. He felt like a person crawling out of a desert who was handed a beaker of cool water only for it to be snatched from his lips.

But if he couldn't forget, then the only other option was to avoid the teasing, treacherous rip currents of desire that seemed intent on pulling him under. His eyes fixed on the pool. Only to do that, he would need to learn how to swim.

Gazing up, Ondine watched transfixed as the coin spun up into the mid-afternoon sunshine. It seemed to hover momentarily as if defying gravity and then, still spinning, it fell back down. Jack caught it. 'Your call.'

'Tails,' she said quickly.

The corners of his mouth curved very slightly. 'Looks like you're going first, Mrs Walcott.'

Jack had invited her to play croquet after lunch and, once he'd explained the rules, including the option to 'roquet' which involved hitting your opponent's ball as far as you could, they were now standing on the immaculate green lawn. Up close, it looked even more perfect, and she had almost winced when Jack had pushed in the wickets.

Now he was handing her one of the long-handled mallets. 'You ready?'

To play croquet: yes.

To play croquet with him: less clear.

What was clear, however, was that she was having to steel herself for every interaction. She tried her hardest to ignore the effect Jack had on her, but it was getting more difficult by the day. It didn't help that he always looked so damn sexy. Today he was wearing chinos, a white button-down and a baseball cap. It was the kind of preppy look favoured by so many of the male guests at Whitecaps that when she was tired they seemed to blur into one person. But there was nothing blurry about Jack Walcott. If he had been a sketch, every angle and contour of his face would have been a clean line.

'Yes, I'm ready.'

As she nodded, he made a small bow. '*Morituri te salutant.* Those who are about to die salute you,' he said softly. 'It's what the gladiators are supposed to have said when they went into the Colosseum.'

She raised an eyebrow. 'Is that you trying to put me off my game?'

He grinned. 'I just want you to be fully prepared.'

'It's croquet, Jack, not *Battle Royale*.'

Still grinning, he backed away from her, shaking his head. 'You clearly have never seen *Heathers*. Croquet is the most brutal, unsporting game you will ever play. Don't say I didn't warn you.'

It pained her to even think it, but he wasn't exaggerating, she thought thirty minutes later as Jack whacked his ball into hers with the force of a door ram to send it spinning out of orbit to the edge of the lawn.

'Sorry.' He grinned, looking about as un-sorry as it was possible to look. 'I was going easy on you before, but I wouldn't be teaching you properly if I didn't demonstrate the correct use of the roquet,' he said, positioning his mallet and then tapping his own ball expertly through the fourth wicket. 'You see, there are two aspects to the game. The physical and the strategic. The best players are strategists.'

The same was true of life, she thought. And given that her strategy was about on a par with pinning a tail on the donkey blindfold, was it any wonder her life was such a mess? Although, strangely, given everything that was going on right now, it felt less messy than it had in a long time.

It took several fruitless, frustrating attempts but at long last she got her ball through the final wicket.

'Well done.'

She turned. Jack was standing behind her clapping slowly. He had pushed the sunglasses to the top of his head and the intensity of his gaze made her skin sting. What was he thinking when he looked at her like that? As if he couldn't look away.

Feeling exposed, she pulled a face. 'Honestly, I don't think any game has ever made me so furious or close to violence.'

He laughed then, softly, a real laugh that made his eyes gleam brighter than the sun, and she could feel the sound pulling her in.

'You're actually pretty good for a beginner. You just need to get a bit more ruthless.' His smile tugged at something loose inside her. 'Like me.'

The sun was behind him, and the light clung to him as greedily as her eyes.

'You're not ruthless.'

'Am I not?'

As his eyes found hers, her stomach knotted fiercely. She had spoken without thinking, prompted by the memory of nights when he had sat with her in the bathroom. Nobody was watching. He could have stayed in his room, but whatever his reason for not doing so, it could hardly be described as ruthless. Instead, he had been kind, and so unfazed that, after the first time, she hadn't felt self-conscious at all. And now here they were playing croquet, and he was a surprisingly good teacher. Relaxed, funny, encouraging. When the time came, he would be a good father.

Her throat tightened. But first he would have to accept that he was one.

Lifting her mallet, she let it swing gently, feeling its weight. True to her word, she hadn't raised the subject of the baby with him since that taut conversation out on the veranda, and it had been easy enough to put it to the back of her mind when she was being sick, but could it seriously stay off-limits for ever?

Then again, what had changed between them? Her morning sickness might have prompted some sort of truce, but one game of croquet didn't mean Jack was any closer to believing he was the father of their baby. Or that he even wanted to co-parent. She couldn't in all honesty say that was what she wanted either. Of course, her ideal would be to raise her child in a close, happy family. But her marriage to Jack was a long way from that ideal.

Crucially it was not based on love or permanence.

'Sometimes,' she said quickly. 'But it can't just be about ruthlessness. Surely there must be something I can do to get better because right now it feels like I'd have as much luck playing with a flamingo.'

She had kept her voice light and jokey, but Jack

didn't laugh, he just stared at her speculatively, and for one horrible moment she thought he was going to ask her why she had defended him. But finally, he nodded slowly and said, 'There are some ways you can improve your swing. Offhand, I'd say you need to keep your head lower when you hit the ball and I think it would help if you loosened your grip.' He hesitated. 'I could show you. If you'll let me.'

The breath jerked in her throat.

It was the first time that he had referred, albeit obliquely, to what had happened yesterday on the beach. She still couldn't quite believe what he had told her. Not just that he couldn't swim but, knowing that, he had still leapt into the sea.

And the reason he'd given for doing so? Did she believe that? She felt the blood in her heart pull back sharply like the tide around a breakwater. Truthfully, she didn't know. Having spent time with him, she could imagine his frustration at finding himself trapped on a yacht, and he was certainly impulsive. She wouldn't be here now if he weren't. And yet she couldn't help but feel that there was more to it.

Maybe she should have pressed him, but she knew how hard it was to reveal your weaknesses to other people. Look at all the things she was keeping hidden from Jack. Only there was no reason to tell him the truth. Particularly when he was still refusing to accept the biggest truth between them.

A small shiver of sadness wound through her. Aside from a baby he wouldn't acknowledge, all that connected them was a piece of paper with some signatures on it.

Her throat was suddenly dry and tight so that it was difficult to swallow.

That was a lie. Out on the beach yesterday, they'd been on the verge of kissing again. At some point between him telling her that all this was 'her life' and her taking his hand, something had shifted. The light dancing off the waves had changed. The breeze had softened. And that thing that they both pretended wasn't there had pulled taut, reeling them closer and closer—

Yes, but only because he had opened up to her, she told herself firmly. And because they had been on a beach again and everything had felt muddled. If she were standing that close to him now, here on this perfectly manicured lawn, it would feel completely different. Neutral.

It was then that she realised that Jack was staring at her and that she had no idea how long he had been waiting for her to reply to him.

'Go on, then. You can show me. On one condition: you join me in the pool later.' Lifting her mallet, she jabbed him lightly in the stomach.

'Oh, and try not to do the whole mansplaining thing.'

His mouth curled into one of those crooked smiles that instantly made her feel as panicky and breathless as a fish on a hook. 'Spoilsport.'

As he stepped closer, she felt her pulse change up a gear. 'Okay, what matters isn't so much how high you grip as the pressure you apply,' he said softly. 'You need to let the wood flow beneath your fingers.'

The hair on the nape of her neck rose as he moved behind her and she felt his cheek next to hers, and then his hands were overlapping hers and he was loosening her fingers, altering her grip around the smooth wooden handle. She tried to focus on what he was saying but it was difficult to concentrate when all she could think about was those same hands moving over her body, their rough urgency making her forget everything but her need for him in that moment.

'Like this,' he said, and his voice was soft and low as it vibrated against her throat. 'Then it's easier to swing. Can you feel it?'

She nodded because she couldn't speak. He was too close and his body was hot, pressed against her back so it felt as if she were melting into him, and she would have stayed like that for ever, with his arms shielding her from the world and his breath mingling with hers, but then she remembered what she had told herself seconds earlier and she slid away from him.

'I see what you mean. Thank you for showing me,' she said, suddenly stiffly polite.

'It was my pleasure. My grandfather is really the expert though.' He reached into his back pocket. 'Which reminds me. We need to take a selfie and send it to him. He'll be chuffed to bits.' He turned to where the housekeeper was putting out a jug of fresh lemonade on the table. 'Sally, could you come and take a photo for us?'

They had taken lots of photos already. At first she had found it awkward and intrusive, not to say unsettling, having to paste a smile on her face and nestle in close to Jack. Now she was more used to it, so it was easier to strike a pose, but still.

'Wait a minute. I just need to—'

Jack frowned. 'You don't need to do anything. You look beautiful.'

It was just words, but she felt a mix of panic and fascination as his golden gaze grazed her face.

'What about if you stand back-to-back?' Sally suggested. 'Lean in on your mallets. Oh, yes, that's super-cute.'

They leaned in, then turned to face one another, and Jack pulled her against him, his hand curving around her waist, his beautiful mouth curling into one of his devastating smiles. 'Thanks,

Sally,' he said, taking back the phone. But as he stared down at the screen, the smile on his face stiffened.

'What is it?'

'Nothing.' He shook his head, recovering his poise. 'They just look a bit staged. Why don't we try—? No, Ondine, no—' But it was too late, she snatched the phone and was staring down at the screen.

'What are you talking about? They look great. I mean, yeah, they look like we posed for them, but that's kinda cute. It looks like we're having fun. I don't see why you don't like them.'

And then she saw why.

For a moment she couldn't breathe. She just stood there, the phone trembling in her hand in time to her pulse as she zoomed in on herself.

She was wearing a vest dress and a cropped cardigan, both from chain stores, but it wasn't her budget wardrobe that had caused Jack to recoil. It was the small but unmistakable outline of a bump pushing against the fabric.

'He doesn't know yet.' Jack's voice pulled her out of her thoughts, and she looked up at him, her throat knotting around a lump of something that was surely too solid to be tears. But why? She knew he felt this way. It was why she'd been avoiding the conversation.

Now, though, she could no longer ignore it because the camera didn't lie.

'He can't find out this way,' Jack said quietly, but firmly. 'I just need some more time—'

Her heart contracted. It was the same impulse that had stopped her from telling her parents about not getting pregnant and Garrett's betrayal. And to be fair, even though she had agreed to do so, she hadn't told Oli about marrying Jack or the pregnancy. But that was different. Her brother might be the smartest, most sensible teenager on the planet, but he was still a teenager who hadn't even had a serious girlfriend yet and it was her job to protect him, not make him anxious about what would look like a shotgun wedding.

And, given her track record with husbands, he would be anxious. Her mouth thinned—and speaking of husbands, she was done with being fair.

'What for?' She gave him a small, stiff smile. 'Just use your legendary powers of persuasion. No, actually, scrap that! I've got a better idea. You could just deny everything.' She couldn't keep the bitterness from her voice. 'You're really good at that.'

His eyes narrowed, the smiling, charming man of moments earlier vanishing before her eyes. 'I can't deny what isn't true and I'm sorry if you don't like that but—'

She suddenly felt sick, only not like before. This wasn't hormones. It was misery and anger and a horrible sense of the wrongness of what she had done, what they were doing.

'No, what I don't like is having this baby edited out before it's even born.'

He flinched, or maybe it was just the light in her eyes because now his lip was curling.

She held up her hand.

'Don't. Just don't, okay? I'm going to lie down. Alone.' And without giving him a chance to reply, she turned and stalked towards the house.

Pushing his plate away, Jack stared across the table at the empty chair where Ondine had sat at breakfast and lunchtime and would have sat this evening if she hadn't sent a message via Sally that she was tired and would be having an early night.

Maybe she was tired, but she was also avoiding him. And punishing him.

Staring down at his uneaten dessert, he had to clench his hands to stop himself from hurling the plate across the room. He had been tempted to storm up to her room and demand that she join him for dinner, but she would undoubtedly refuse and he could hardly force her to join him.

That would defeat the point anyway because what he wanted was for her to want to join him. What he wanted was for it to go back to how it was when they were playing croquet and their eyes would collide with the same force as if they were trying to roquet one another only instead of pushing them further apart, it seemed to pull them closer.

Until Sally had taken those photos, and he had reacted, *understandably*, he thought with a stab of frustration, only Ondine had got all out of shape, just as she had on the bluffs. Except this time she hadn't come back. And he missed her—

No, not that. Never that.

He pushed back his chair and got to his feet, moving swiftly out of the room and through the quiet house, panic swelling against his solar plexus.

It was her fault. *Ondine.* If she hadn't got pregnant, then all of this would have been so much more straightforward. It would have stayed transactional. But then she'd started being sick and he had tried to do the right thing, only that meant it was no longer just about the appearance of things and the money.

She had started to trust him. Worse, he'd started to trust her and he'd ended up telling her about not being able to swim and suddenly he was teaching her croquet.

His body tensed as he remembered the curve of her spine against his chest, and the sudden quickening of hunger he had felt. It had been nearly impossible to resist… His mouth thinned. And impossible to deny despite his alleged expertise in that area.

He came to an abrupt stop, his pulse jerking in his throat, somewhat surprised to find that he had made his way to the indoor pool. Gazing down, he felt a vertiginous rush of blood just as he had on the yacht. But this wasn't the sea. The water was waveless and clear. He could see the tiles on the bottom. He had strength and stamina. How hard could it be?

'Don't even think about it.'

His head snapped round, and now his pulse was beating out of time for a different reason. Ondine was hovering in the doorway, still wearing the sundress from earlier. Her face was pale and wary as if she wasn't sure of her reception, but she had said she would join him in the pool, and here she was.

'I wasn't going to jump,' he said slowly. Couldn't, not wasn't. He wanted to beat this stupid, irrational fear but he didn't know how on his own. Only he wasn't on his own, he thought as Ondine walked towards him.

'Good,' she said quietly. 'Because there are rules to follow around water.' She stopped in front of him, her blue eyes resting steadily on his face. 'And if I'm going to teach you to swim, you're going to have to follow them. And the first rule for any beginner is that you don't go into the water alone.'

'Not even the shower?' he said softly for the incomparable pleasure of watching her try and stop her mouth pulling up at the corners. But this time her mouth didn't move. Instead, her eyes locked with his and then she pulled her dress up and over her head.

Jack felt his body fill with a kind of stillness as if every pulsing, beating part had abruptly malfunctioned. And maybe it had, he thought, gazing down, dry-mouthed, at Ondine. She was wearing what amounted to four small triangles of burnt orange-coloured fabric. To be fair, he could only see three, but he imagined— Actually he didn't want to let his imagination into this conversation.

'On this occasion, you'll be going in with me and I will be in touching distance at all times. Do you think you can remember that, Jack?'

His eyes roamed over the three triangles and he nodded, then cleared his throat. 'Yes, I can remember that.'

'Then I suggest you get changed.'

CHAPTER EIGHT

SHE WAS A good teacher. Patient. Precise. Emphatic but not overbearing. As if she spent every waking hour teaching men in their thirties how to make star shapes in the water. Maybe that was why he was not embarrassed as he'd imagined he would be whenever he'd pictured himself learning to swim.

It also helped that, as she'd predicted, he was a quick learner so that within half an hour he was pushing off from the wall of the pool and doing a fairly competent doggy-paddle.

'So who else have you taught to swim?'

They were in the shallow end now, sitting on the steps. It was the first time he could remember allowing himself to relax in water. Normally, he was too tense about someone pulling him for a joke, but he felt safe with Ondine.

'Children mostly. But plenty of adults too. You're not alone.' Their eyes met, and she gave him one of those careful smiles.

'Were you always a good swimmer? Like, when you were a kid?'

Earlier in the pool, he had congratulated himself for being so focused on her instructions. But then, only her head and shoulders were out of the water. Now though, as she nodded, he was suddenly intensely conscious of her almost nakedness, and of the excitement leaping inside him.

'I did Swim Club, but I did a lot of clubs when I was younger.' She hesitated. 'I wasn't very academic, you see. Not like Oli. And my parents knew that I minded.' Her smile softened a little. 'They enrolled me in all these different activities so that I could find something I was really good at.'

'And that was swimming.' He dragged his gaze up and away from a droplet of water that was zigzagging between the smooth, damp skin of her cleavage.

Her mouth twitched at the corner. 'It wasn't playing the violin, that's for sure.'

'And after Swim Club?' He wanted her to keep talking, to keep watching her talk.

'I got selected for the junior swim team. The coaches were amazing. Some of the people I trained with swam in international competitions But I injured my shoulder.'

'That was bad luck.'

She shrugged. 'It happens. I'm over it now, but I would have liked to make my parents proud.'

There was a wistful note in her voice, and he frowned. 'You save lives. I'm pretty sure that would make them prouder than any medal.'

His shoulders stiffened; this was dangerous territory for him. But glancing over, he saw a tension in Ondine that matched his own.

'They would be.' She rubbed her forehead with the back of his hand. 'But they died before I finished my training.'

Died? Jack swore silently. 'I'm sorry.'

She was shaking her head. 'It's fine. You didn't know.'

But he should have done. The marriage might be fake but Ondine was a real person, and losing your parents was a huge, life-changing moment at any age, only she was so young.

'That must have been hard,' he said quietly.

'It was. That's why Oli lives with me. He had to—he was only fourteen. And I wanted him to,' she added, her blue eyes widening as if that weren't obvious.

'I know.' He thought about how her voice softened when she talked about her brother, and the small, shabby home he'd judged and found wanting. He'd done the same to her. But the inadequacy was his, not hers: she was working two jobs to help raise her brother.

'Is that why you have no money?'

She looked down into her lap. 'No,' she said finally, and there was a flatness to her voice now that he hated, but not as much as he hated himself. 'That's down to me and my ex-husband. The second one, I mean.'

His anger was instant and so intense that for a moment he couldn't speak. 'What did he do?'

'I don't know why I said that.' She was shaking her head. 'Vince wasn't to blame. I mean, he was. He liked having fun, but I knew that right from the start. He didn't hide who he was, and it was my choice to marry him.'

'Did you love him?' His heart scraped against his ribs.

Her mouth trembled. 'No, I don't think I did, but we met just after my parents' funeral and Vince could see how miserable I was, and he's like a big, stupid dog that just wants you to be happy. But he's not a grown-up. I knew that, and I still married him.'

Jack stared at her uncertainly. He felt out of his depth. Normally, this kind of conversation was his cue to leave but he didn't want to leave Ondine. In fact, he wanted to get closer. 'You were grieving. People do all kinds of crazy stuff when they're in pain.' Look at me, he wanted to say but instead he reached out and took her hand, but she jerked it away, shaking her head.

'You don't understand. I married him because I was scared and sad, and Vince made me laugh. He made me forget. And I wanted to forget. I wanted to have fun and I wanted Oli to have fun. To have nice things. I didn't think about the future or what the money was supposed to be for.

Only then the bills started to come in and it was like I woke up. Or maybe I grew up.'

He heard and hated the guilt in her voice. 'What did you do?'

'I told him to leave, and he did. We got divorced and I got the job at Whitecaps. I was managing just fine, but then after you left that day Vince rang and he told me that Oli's college fund was gone.' She swallowed. 'I rang Stanford. I thought I might be able to get a bursary but there was nothing they could do, and the bank wouldn't give me a loan—not one that would cover the fees anyway.'

And now he understood why she had come to the bungalow. 'That's why you changed your mind. Why you came to find me.'

His voice was steady but inside he was knocked sideways by the truth. That the money was for Oli because Ondine felt responsible, and she had acted on that feeling with the fierce, unthinking selflessness of a mother protecting her cub, throwing aside her clear and understandable reservations to marry a stranger for money. And he had judged her for it; been happy to judge her just as people judged him, even when it became obvious that the woman sitting beside him was incapable of living the lie he had told himself.

He felt hot with shame. His head was a swirling carousel of all the other lies he'd told himself to make his life work, truths he needed to keep hidden, questions he couldn't ask much less answer. Reaching out, he caught hold of the one solid fact.

'You wanted the money for your brother.'

She nodded. 'He's lost so much already. I couldn't take away his future as well.'

He could feel the pain in her voice inside his chest and he reached for her hand again, and this time she let him take it. 'You haven't taken anything away. You've given him a home, and love—'

'I let him down. I'm supposed to take care of him but I was stupid and careless and selfish—'

'You're not any of those things.' Jack pulled her against him. 'You're tough and brave and loyal and hard-working, and Oli is lucky to have you.'

She cried then, and he held her close until finally, she breathed out shakily and then he slid his hand under her chin, and tilted her head back so that she was looking up into his eyes. 'You don't have to worry about money, okay? You're with me now, and I can take care of you and the baby, and Oli. Whatever you need, it's yours.'

'You don't have to do that. In fact, you shouldn't do it.' Her voice was scratchy when she answered. 'Marrying me is supposed to have stopped you making impulsive decisions.'

There was silence. Her pulse was hammering against the delicate skin of her throat.

'You make me impulsive,' he said softly. He
watched her shift against the tiles, a pink bloom
colouring her cheeks. And then, as if to prove
his point, he leaned forward and fitted his mouth
to hers.

He felt her lips stiffen, and his brain froze with
panic that he had got it completely wrong, that
the shimmering heat between them was a mirage
of his own creation, but then she captured his
face in her hands and she was kissing him back,
her lips soft and eager, and the taste of her was
sweeter than honey.

And he just wanted a taste. Except he didn't.
Now that she was in his arms, he wanted to touch
her and press his body against hers and he knew
that he should pull away. Kiss her forehead. Make
an excuse about boundaries but he couldn't make
himself do that. Only why? Why did her kiss
make him feel like this, so full of hunger, and
heat and wanting her?

But then her hands slid over his chest and his
mind was nothing but heat and, reaching down,
he scooped her into his arms and carried her out
of the pool.

Breaking the kiss, he lowered her onto the
lounger. His whole body was pulsing with a need
that was turning him inside out so that he could
have taken her there and then, like before, but he

hadn't taken time to savour that miraculous body and he forced himself to slow.

He lowered his mouth to her breast. The nipple was already stiff against the wet fabric and he sucked it into his mouth, and immediately his decision to go slow was put to the test as she arched upwards, moaning softly. Breathing unsteadily, he abandoned her breast to kiss her on the mouth again, parting her lips, tasting her again and then he licked a path down to her other breast, pushing the triangles of fabric up so that he could suck the bare, ruched tip.

Her hand was in his hair, twitching against his scalp as he licked and sucked and she was pulling down his swim shorts, freeing him into the warm air.

'Yes—' He clenched his teeth, hips jerking forward as she wrapped her hand around the already stone-hard length of his erection. And then his hand caught her hair, gripping it reflexively as she took him into her mouth and he sucked in a breath, lost. The feel of her tongue, so and sweet and irresistible.

Gazing up at Jack's face, Ondine felt her already hypersensitive nipples tighten painfully. She had really enjoyed this before but, with Jack, the desire to taste him was overwhelming, his pleasure gave her pleasure, she thought, her tongue flicking over the smooth, velvet-soft skin, feeling the blood pulsing beneath the tip—

He made a raw sound in his throat and now he shifted backwards, and she stared up at him, a pulse beating hard between her thighs. He had stood in front of her like this in her dreams. Naked. Unashamed. Beautiful. And aroused. But reality was even better than fantasy, she thought, gazing at the taut body and his hard, thick, pulsing erection. He was beautiful and aroused.

Very aroused.

She watched, mesmerised, as he slowly knelt at the end of the lounger, his dark glittering gaze trained on her face as he slid his hands under her bikini bottoms and drew them down her legs. He hesitated and then he reached up and touched her belly gently, reverentially, his fingers soft and light and magical, stroking her, stirring her, his touch melting her inside.

Now his hands moved across her thighs, sliding slowly between them, and then he lowered his mouth, trailing fire across the soft skin so she arched upwards, wanting more, wanting the ache between her thighs answered now.

Quivers of anticipation rippled across her skin and then he gently parted her legs and kissed where she was warm and slick and ready, his tongue seeking her clitoris. And the tip of his tongue… She whimpered. Oh, God, she hadn't known anything could feel so good. She was hollowed out with need, shaking inside and out, her breasts aching so that it was almost too painful to bear, and then she pressed herself closer, her head falling back against the lounger as her body splintered apart, and she was crying out, crying out his name.

She felt him shift, reach for her, his mouth seeking hers, kissing her and she was reaching for him, pressing his erection against the quivering heat between her thighs.

'Are you sure?' he said hoarsely. His eyes flicked down to her stomach. 'I can—'

'No.' She shook her head. 'I want to feel you—'

He moved forward, his golden eyes burning fiercely, and he kissed her for a long time and then he touched her between her thighs, stroking her, opening her and then he lifted her hips and he was there, hard against her, sliding in, inch by inch, stretching her—

Her pulse quickened as he shifted his weight, lifting her hips, moving inside her in a steady, intoxicating rhythm and all the time he was getting bigger and harder and she could feel herself tightening on the inside, muscles clenching, head spinning, trying to hold onto the heat of him.

His fingers tightened around her hips and then she felt him tense and she couldn't hold back the moan of pleasure as he thrust deeper, and she was grasping his hands where they held her, her body shuddering into spasms as he surged inside her.

For a moment, he stood there, hips jerking and then, breathing out raggedly, he lowered her down and she felt him pull out. Seconds later, he lay down beside her, gathering her into his arms.

Ondine buried her face against his shoulder. She could feel his heartbeat slamming into her ribs. She couldn't bring herself to open her eyes. She just wanted to stay there, breathing in the warm scent of his skin, the hard swell of his biceps keeping everything at bay. She felt his lips brush against her hair.

'It's okay, baby, it's okay.'

Was it?

In one way, the most obvious, most literal way, it was not just okay, it was amazing. Sex with Jack was a thing of wonder and beauty. It was mind-melting, dizzyingly sublime. What was less okay was that what just happened was not some feverish hook-up that could be written off as a heat-of-the-moment impulse, it was a conscious choice, for both of them.

That was if something that had been coming since the day she'd thrown him out of her house could be described as a choice.

She lifted her face. Jack was staring at her, his pupils huge and dark.

'I didn't hurt you, did I?' he said hoarsely.

Her lips felt puffy, her mouth bruised from kissing him and, breathing out shakily, she found she couldn't speak and she shook her head. It was the truth. He hadn't hurt her. But he had changed her.

Their first time together had been an explosive solar flare of hunger, a white heat of mutual need consuming them both. But this was slower, sharper, pulling everything into focus, unlocking something inside her so unashamedly sexual that she didn't know herself. Every touch, every caress, every lick seemed to shape a new understanding of who she was, who she could be, who she wanted to be.

Lying here now, with his fever-hot skin pressing into hers, everything felt so intense, so vivid. It was as if she were newly born, and seeing colour, objects, for the first time. She could hear Jack's heart beating inside her and her body felt smooth and soft, and so sensitive, and it was because of Jack. He had done this. This man who was a stranger when she married him had changed her for ever in all the ways she had assumed marriage and sex would change a person, but had never happened with either of her first two husbands.

'Are you sure?'

Suddenly close to tears, she jolted back to him, back to the shimmering golden haze of his eyes

and the streaks of colour touching his hard cheekbones.

As she met his gaze, she felt a kick of panic.
Was he regretting it? She stared at him, trying
to take in each curve and line of his astonishing
face, her heart shuddering as if he had reached inside her chest and started squeezing it in his fist.

Please, don't let him regret it—

'Yes, I'm sure. You didn't hurt me.'

He was on his side, still watching her. 'It's just
so different with you. I don't...' He hesitated, his
mouth twisting into a shape she didn't recognise.
Not anger or confusion but something in between.
'I couldn't hold back—'

The tears that seemed to be clogging her throat
pushed up and as she gazed up into his flushed,
shocked face her vision blurred—

Swearing softly, he pulled her against the hard
muscles of his chest, his hand soft in her hair.
She held onto him, not moving, hardly breathing.

'Don't cry. I don't ever want to make you
cry—'

There was an ache in his voice, and now he
spoke quickly, the words spilling from his beautiful mouth. She reached up and pressed her finger to his lips.

'It's not you...it's not you...'

Not *just* you, she should have said. Jack was
there at the top of the list. How could he not be?

From the moment he'd jumped off that yacht, her life had not been her own. It was as if she were a kite and he were pulling the strings, making her twist and tumble in a sky as blue and endless as the sea.

But there was losing her mum and dad too and wanting but struggling to be any kind of substitute parent for Oli. And all the months of trying and failing to get pregnant ending in Garrett's betrayal, and then the stupidity of her second marriage to Vince.

And all of it had begun so quickly and in such a disconnected, haphazard way; there was never any time to think properly about what she wanted to happen, what she should do, and she had made so many mistakes, thrown away so many opportunities—

'It's just so much has happened—' So much he didn't even know about, and now it was her turn to hesitate.

He let out a long breath. 'I know.'

'And now there's you and—'

She was about to say *and the baby*, but the coward in her knew that she would have to get up and leave if he rejected their child in this most intimate of moments, and she couldn't bear to do that. 'There's this—'

She felt his heartbeat accelerate against her

ribs, felt his hand tighten in her hair. 'Are you saying you regret it?'

'No. I'm not. I don't regret it, at all. Do you?' She knew she should be trying to hide the note of panic, but her voice wouldn't co-operate.

His gold eyes were the darkest she'd ever seen them.

'No.' Shaking his head, he lowered his mouth and kissed her fiercely, not just her lips but her cheeks and her forehead, the curve of her jaw and the hollow of her throat. 'I've never wanted any woman more than I want you. You make me feel things I've never felt, never wanted to feel.'

He frowned then as if he'd said too much and, reaching up, she touched his face lightly, marvelling at its smoothness and symmetry. 'I feel the same way,' she whispered.

For a moment they stared at one another and then she was leaning in and kissing him and his hands were cupping her breasts, grazing the nipples and the sensation was so sharp and intense that she squirmed against him, her body rippling to life all over again.

Ondine woke, slowly, reluctantly, blinking into the soft yellow sunlight that was spilling in through the window between the half-open curtains. At some point in the night she and Jack had left the pool house and made their way through the silent, watchful house upstairs to the bedroom, to the bed they were supposed to share, but never had.

There had been no awkward moment as they'd reached the bedroom door. She had simply opened it and led him inside and he had pushed it shut, reaching for her as he did so. And they had kept reaching for one another as the darkness around them deepened to the colour of spilt ink, again and again, until finally the sky started to lighten through all the shades of grey.

Now, though, she was alone, and even though she knew it was stupid to mind, Jack's absence seemed to have opened up some hollow in her chest.

Rolling onto her side, she reached over and pressed the flat of her hand against the mattress. She'd known he was gone the moment she woke up. Known it even before she'd opened her eyes. But maybe that was just what he did after he spent the night with a woman.

She frowned. She was making it sound like a one-night stand. But that didn't make any sense because they were married. Surely you had a one-night stand with someone you didn't know. Then again, what did she know? She'd only had three sexual partners, and she had ended up marrying all of them.

It made her feel off balance bracketing them

together in that way because they were all very different. For starters, she had believed she was in love with Garrett and Vince, but the thought of love had never entered her mind with Jack.

And yet it was Jack whose touch made her shiver all the way through. Jack who made her melt on the inside. Jack who had claimed her body. And not just her body, she thought, remembering last night's tearful confession. She had never told either of her ex-husbands anything that deeply personal. Maybe that was why him being here in this bed, their bed, felt so right.

Staring blindly across the room, she saw the sun disappear behind a cloud. Or maybe she was just tired and hormonal because she had been here before.

Twice.

With Garrett, she had fallen for his certainty, trusting, expecting him to be steadfast and true. And because Vince made her laugh, she had assumed he would make her happy. Now she was doing the same thing with Jack, wanting this encounter to mean something more than bodies and skin and sweat.

She glanced down at the tangle of bedsheets.

But this was sex. Wild, sublime, incomparable sex; she doubted that any man would ever make her feel as alive and aware and as beautiful in his bed as Jack. And yet, she knew it wasn't enough.

The truth was that the relationships that worked,
like her parents', were more than just a chemical attraction.

Her hand moved protectively to her stomach
where once there had been an indent and now
there was a bump. And anyway, this relationship
was about more than just her and Jack.

She thought back to what he'd said about taking care of her and Oli and the baby. He meant
financially, and of course she wasn't going to pretend that Jack's money wouldn't make a difference. How could she? It was making a difference
right now. And she knew he was trying to help,
trying to reassure her. But it was not an acknowl-
edgement that this baby was his any more than
his concern during sex. Remembering how he'd
wanted to edit all evidence of her ongoing pregnancy from the photos on his phone, she felt her
throat tighten. He was still a long way from acknowledging that.

Which was why, up until now, she had pushed
Jack's postpartum involvement in their baby's life
to a corner of her mind she didn't visit very often.

Her fingers flexed against her abdomen.

Sometimes she wondered if she had tried hard
enough to make him believe her. There were moments when she had thought about telling him
about Garrett and the agonising months of disappointment and despair, as if that might prove

she wasn't the manipulative little hustler he'd accused her of being. Once or twice she even felt the words form into sentences, but the pain and shame of those months were so embedded in the fascia of her body that she couldn't say them out loud.

And it had been easier before not to rock the boat.

But what about now?

'Penny for them?'

Ondine blinked. Jack was standing in the doorway. His handsome face was calm and blank, but his eyes were watching her with a lazy, predatory gleam that made her breath tangle in her throat. He was wearing loose black shorts and a black vest and his skin was flushed from working out, although how he had the energy was beyond her.

Not that she was complaining about the end results, she thought as her gaze roamed over the smooth muscles of his arms and chest.

'I was just wondering what time it is.' She shifted up the bed but as she did so the sheet fell away from her body and she felt his dark gold gaze move over her breasts with the same freedom his hands had in the hours before dawn.

So now they were both staring at each other like moonstruck idiots.

Jack recovered first.

'I'm not actually sure.' He walked across the room and stopped at the end of the bed, his fingers flexing round the top rail as if it were a barbell. 'Somewhere between brunch and lunch.'

She laughed. 'I'm guessing that means you're hungry.'

His gaze was steady and unwavering. 'It's hard not to be when I'm around you,' he said, after a moment. 'You make me hungry.' She felt her body react, skin tightening, breasts tingling, nipples suddenly incredibly sensitive. It was an echo of what he'd said to her in the pool house last night—was it really only last night?—and it was all too easy to remember what had happened afterwards. All too tempting to turn memory into a live action replay.

'And you make me greedy,' she said quietly.

He was still watching her and she felt his gaze, felt the intensity of his concentration. 'I'm glad you've got your appetite back. The doctor will be too.'

She tilted her head back to meet his eyes. 'I think she was talking about food. Not sex.'

His dense, dark lashes snapped upwards at the directness of her words. 'But you are. Talking about sex, I mean.'

'Yes.' Heart thudding, she pulled the sheet up to cover herself. 'We both are. Except we're not talking about it. We're tiptoeing round it—'

His gaze sharpened. 'I see. And you want us to be less coy?'

'Don't you? Or do you just want to pretend it never happened?' The bitterness in her voice echoed around the bedroom.

There was a silence. His eyes narrowed. 'That's not what I said.'

It wasn't. 'I know.'

'But I could see why you might think it's what I meant.'

Their eyes met. Jack was still standing at the end of the bed, still tall and astonishingly, shockingly beautiful, but he looked serious now and yet also younger. It reminded her of when they were out on the bluff.

'You can?' she said slowly.

He nodded. 'Being married like this, it's been harder than either of us thought. And any part that's been made more challenging is almost certainly my fault. I have a lot of faults, as you've probably realised.' He gave her a small, tight smile. 'But I'm not a total idiot. Or a monster.'

'I don't think you're an idiot or a monster. I just think we should talk about what happened. Only I'm not very good at this kind of conversation.'

'And you think I am?' He hesitated, and then he walked round to where she was hunched against the pillows and sat down beside her on the bed.

'Well, you've dated more than two people, so, yes, I would hope so.' She shivered, her nerves ambushed by a sudden spasm of misery imagining Jack's multiple conquests. 'It's just that last night, we said some things. And I meant what I said, and I thought you did too but then when I woke up this morning you'd gone and so I thought maybe I'd got it wrong. That it wasn't real—'

'You think I faked that?' He seemed stunned.

She frowned. 'I don't mean the mechanics. You made it sound as if you wanted me, wanted to have sex with me—'

'I did.' His voice was hoarse. 'I do. I guess I didn't want to assume— No, actually that's a lie. When I woke up this morning I wanted to make all kinds of assumptions.' His eyes fixed on her face. 'One of them was that we could just carry on without having to talk about it.' Reaching out, he uncurled her fingers and slid his hand around hers. 'But what I should have done was tell you the truth. That I wanted you since that very first day when you kicked me out of your house. And I want you now.'

Her body ached with need.

'You're not worried about it making things more complicated?'

'I think we passed complicated a long time ago,' he said softly, and, leaning forward, he fitted his mouth to hers.

For a moment they kissed, back and forth, teasing the heat from each other, then she felt him tense. 'What is it?'

'I worked out pretty hard in the gym. I definitely need to shower.' He grimaced. 'You can't want me like this.'

She did. The scent of his sweat was tugging at her senses. Then again—

Picturing Jack with water spilling over all those glorious curving muscles, she felt a shiver of anticipation dance across her skin.

'So take a shower.' Still clutching the sheet, she stood up.

'What are you doing?' His gaze had risen to meet hers and now she let the sheet drop and his eyes seemed to glow as they fixed on her naked body.

'Coming with you.' Hunger jackknifed inside her. 'I can't let you go into the water alone. Or did you forget the rules?'

She managed two steps before he caught up with her, making her shriek with laughter as he scooped her into his arms and carried her into the bathroom.

CHAPTER NINE

Shifting back in his chair, Jack stared at his laptop and reread the final line of text on the screen. The proposal was finished. He was just tinkering with it. What he should be doing was sending it to his grandfather, but he wasn't ready to do that yet. And yet he couldn't leave it alone either so now he was carrying his laptop around with him everywhere like a security blanket.

Not that he needed one. He felt calmer than he had in years, decades even, and happy. But then he had a lot to be happy about. His plan was working, more than working, he thought, glancing through the window.

Outside in the garden, Ondine was standing on the croquet lawn, practising her swing, her forehead creased with concentration, her light brown hair spilling across her shoulders. The same shoulders he'd kissed and licked earlier as she'd leaned forward, moaning softly, hands splayed against the shower wall. Remembering what had happened next, he felt his groin harden.

On waking, he had been shocked to find Ondine's soft body curled so trustingly against him. More shocking still had been how right it had felt. It was that rightness or rather his panic at seeing it in those terms that had made him slip from the bed and make his way to the gym.

He hadn't booked a session with Mark, but he had pounded the punchbag for thirty minutes then hit the treadmill for another fifty. But he couldn't keep away.

His eyes narrowed. Sally was on the lawn now, talking to Ondine. He watched them smile and laugh. All the staff liked her, and, having worked in hospitality, no doubt Ondine felt some kind of kinship.

But she was also a good person.

He felt a pang of guilt sharpen its point beneath his ribs. He hadn't given a thought to what she would feel like waking alone. Nor had he considered talking to her about what had started in the pool house last night.

Do you just want to pretend it never happened?

No, he hadn't wanted that. But he hadn't wanted to have a conversation that might reveal that fact because he was a coward. Because he was scared of what he might say. Because he couldn't admit to Ondine or himself that he wanted more than just one night with her. Wanting might lead to needing, and needing made you vulnerable.

But she was braver, *better* than him. When life knocked her down, she didn't just get back up, she tried to do the right thing.

Remembering how he had tried to edit out her baby bump from the photos, he felt his chest tighten. He had told her he would take care of her and the baby, but did she think he was going to pretend that had never happened too? More likely, she thought it would be beyond him. And that was entirely understandable. He could hardly manage his own life. Mismanage would be a better description, he thought, remembering the moment when he'd jumped off the yacht.

The memory cast a shadow across his thoughts. He was such a mess. Who would want him in their baby's life? His throat constricted. What if he was not just damaged, but damaging?

He pushed the question aside as he had done so many times before. This wasn't about him. It was about Ondine and making her feel safe. It was time to show her that she could trust him, that he could do the right thing, and, reaching into his pocket, he pulled out his phone.

'I thought you were on some kind of leave?'

Glancing up from his laptop, Jack stared blankly over to where Ondine lay on her side, watching him. They were lounging by the pool. Through the glass, the sun shimmered in a cloudless sky. But no blue in nature could match the beauty of Ondine's eyes.

Eyes that were now fixed steadily on his face.

Shutting his laptop, he turned to face her. 'Well, according to the WEC website, I'm currently "taking a short sabbatical to focus on personal goals". So probably everyone thinks I'm in rehab.'

He unleashed a small, curving smile, hoping to distract her, but her blue gaze stayed steady because, as he already knew, Ondine didn't get distracted easily. Lifeguard training, probably, he thought, his own gaze flickering appreciatively over her toned limbs. She was wearing another of those barely-there bikinis that theoretically should offer little to the imagination but in his case offered rather too much.

'So what are you doing on that?' she said, tapping the laptop. 'Must be pretty enthralling. I've never seen you so focused. Well, you know, aside from—' A flush of pink crept over her cheeks, and he felt his skin tighten. Yes, he knew—

'It's nothing, really. Just something I've been working on.'

'Is that all you're going to tell me?'

'No, I just didn't know if you wanted to get into the details.'

She rolled her eyes. 'I think I can manage. Or is it a secret?'

'No.' He shook his head. 'It's not a secret.' But he never liked to show people that he cared, and he did care very much about this proposal. Then he remembered the ache in Ondine's voice when she told him about her parents, and her ex-husband, and he knew how much it must have cost her to share that with him.

Surely, he could share this.

'It's a kind of side project. A proposal to accelerate WEC's transition from fossil fuels to renewables. We're moving at a glacial pace, the whole industry is. But in five years' time, energy will look nothing like it does now. Green hydrogen. Solar. Hydropower. Geothermals. They'll be the present, not the future. Any business that doesn't get that is going to be left behind. That's why I want to push WEC to transition now.'

He saw a flicker of curiosity in her blue eyes like a wave out at sea. 'Doesn't sound much like a side project.' She glanced at the laptop. 'Could I read it? Would you mind?'

She wanted to read it. He stared at her in silence. Was she joking? But then she held out her hand. 'No, I don't mind. But don't feel like you have to.'

'I don't—'

It took her just over an hour. At one point, watching her chew her lip, he said, 'Honestly, you don't need to read the whole thing—' and she looked up, glowering at the interruption.

Now she closed the laptop. 'It's really good. I didn't have a clue about renewables before, but you made it really accessible. And exciting. So what does your grandfather think?'

He shrugged. 'It's not that he's resistant to change, it's just that, for him, WEC has always been about oil and gas.'

'Did you have a falling out? Is that why you walked out?'

Picturing that life-changing meeting with his grandfather, he felt his stomach churn with a familiar mix of regret and defiance.

'I didn't walk out. My grandfather told me to leave because I skim-read a geological report and there was a problem that we had to pay our way out of. So I never got to show him the proposal, and who knows when he'll be ready to listen to me again?'

His throat clenched as he anticipated Ondine's appraising gaze, her disappointment. 'I know what you're thinking. That it's my fault. That I messed up.'

'Everyone messes up, Jack.' She frowned. 'Even your grandfather.'

'Yeah, well, it wasn't the first time. That's why he sent me away.'

She was quiet for so long, her voice was almost a shock when finally she said, 'You make it sound like a punishment. I don't think it was. He sent you away because he thinks you're good enough to step into his shoes but he wants you to

be fit for race day. And that means taking stock
and being honest with yourself, about what you
need to do to improve. He did what any good
coach would do.'

'And what do you think?'

'Me?' Her eyes fluttered up to meet his.

He nodded. 'You're my wife. Do you think I'm
good enough?' And suddenly there was nothing
more important than to know her answer to that
question.

'Before, no.' She hesitated, and then she smiled,
a smile that filled him with wonder and hope.
'But now, I think you might just pull it off.'

She gave a squeak as he jerked her off the sun
lounge and onto his lap. 'And I think you and my
grandpa are going to get along very well. Maybe
too well.' He paused. Her eyes were soft, open,
trusting, and quickly, before he could change his
mind, he said, 'I talked to him. Earlier. I told him
about the baby.'

She blinked. 'Did it go okay?'

The call had been both easier and harder than
he'd thought it would be, only not for the reasons
he'd imagined. He'd assumed it would be hard
to lie again, but it hadn't felt like a lie. Listening
to the happiness in his grandfather's voice, he'd
forgotten about the condom, and his suspicions
about the timing of the pregnancy. All of it had retreated, and he had simply been happy and whole.

Now, though, gazing down into Ondine's face, he felt the fault lines inside him fracture. She cared about him only because she didn't know the truth. But if, make that *when*, he messed up, she would end up hating him, blaming him.

Pushing aside that thought, he cleared his throat.

'It went well. He's looking forward to meeting you at the polo. They all are.' That wasn't strictly true. He'd left messages with both his parents telling them he had news to share and that he hoped they could join him and Ondine for dinner after the tournament, but neither of them had responded. Not that he had expected them to.

'They?' She looked suddenly nervous.

'My parents. And their partners. My half-siblings.'

She grimaced. 'They certainly won't be able to miss me. I cleared tables at Whitecaps, so I know exactly what kind of women go to polo matches and I don't look like any of them.'

'That's because your beauty is real, not the result of surgery or fillers. Especially now.' He glanced down at the swell of her stomach, his pulse jerking. 'Pregnancy suits you.'

She smiled. 'You clearly have a very short memory.'

Their eyes met, both of them remembering those nights in the bathroom.

'I don't know, you were so determined. That's pretty sexy.' And she was blooming now, he thought, his gaze taking in her flushed cheeks and shining eyes.

'Did you not want children?'

He felt her whole body stiffen and the smile on her face seemed to slip sideways. 'Yes. I did. I wanted to have them with Garrett, my first husband. And we tried for so long.' Her voice stumbled. 'But nothing happened.'

Thinking back to her small, pale face when she'd handed him the positive test, it was suddenly difficult to catch his breath. She'd said it was a miracle, but by then he'd been consumed with a rage that had blocked out compassion or reason.

'Actually, it did happen for Garrett, just not with me.' She rubbed her forehead as if it hurt. Maybe it did. He could certainly feel her pain. 'He had an affair with a woman at work, and she got pregnant and then he left me.'

Glancing past her at the huge trees standing like sentinels at the edge of the gardens, Jack felt a flicker of rage. He wanted to uproot them all and smash them into firewood with his fists. What kind of man would do that?

'I think I would have been okay but then my parents were killed and it got kind of muddled up, you know, grieving for them, worrying about Oli—'

His arms tightened around her. 'I'm so sorry, Ondine.'

Now he didn't want to smash things, he wanted to sit and hold her close for ever. Protect her from the world and its random cruelties.

'It's fine. I'm fine now. I was angry before. With Garrett, and Vince, but I'm not any more.' She seemed confused, as if she had only just re-alised that fact. 'I don't know what changed, but I'm glad it did. They're behind me now.'

'What about after Vince?'

'There hasn't been anyone.' Her eyes were clear and blue; she was telling the truth, but if that was true—

Something was creeping up behind him like in a game of grandmother's footsteps. He felt goose-bumps on his neck.

'But what about the condoms? Why would you have those if there hasn't been anyone?'

'I didn't even know I had them. They must have been from when I was with Garrett. But we stopped using them when we started trying for a baby—'

'When was that?'

'Seven years ago maybe.' Her voice was so faint now he could barely hear it. 'I was on the pill with Vince. I came off it when we broke up because I couldn't handle another relationship.'

Jack stared at her in silence, his heart hammering. He didn't know the expiry time on a condom but he was pretty sure it wasn't seven years. He felt the air quiver as if a giant, underground explosion had happened beneath their feet. But it was inside his chest.

This baby was his. His lungs were burning. He couldn't, *shouldn't* be a father. But he was. He felt a rush of panic and fear and then a joy that scared him more. He heard her swallow, knew she was watching him, and he knew that his face must be showing his shock. His understanding.

'I didn't think I could get pregnant. And I know you feel differently, but I can't regret this baby.' Looking down into her face, he felt something tear inside her. The shine had gone from her eyes. She looked small and lost. Because of him.

'It's okay. We'll work it out.' He pulled her closer, his head spinning. 'It'll be okay,' he repeated, and he kept repeating it like a mantra.

Since its inaugural match nearly fifty years ago, the annual Walcott Cup had become one of those dates in the diary that was not an official holiday but was often treated as such. For football fans, the second Sunday in February was Super Bowl Sunday. Those who preferred to mix equine talent with the chance to dress up, the first Saturday in May was reserved for John D. Walcott IV's charity polo tournament.

Normally, Jack looked forward to the tournament. He enjoyed playing and watching polo, and he was proud of what his grandfather had created. What had started out as an impromptu match between friends now raised millions of dollars for charity.

But this year, he had more important things on his mind than polo. Heart twisting, he glanced over to where Ondine sat opposite him, her eyes fixed on the view outside her window.

It was twenty-four hours since he'd worked out that he was the father of the baby in her womb. Worked out. Accepted. But not acknowledged. Not out loud anyway. So in that sense nothing had changed outwardly.

But everything had changed. All changed… changed utterly, like that Yeats poem his grandfather loved so much.

He had held her close for a long time but they hadn't talked again. Instead they had walked in silence back to the bedroom and reached for one another wordlessly.

There had been no words to express the chaos inside his head. There still weren't any.

And maybe Ondine felt the same way too.

She hadn't changed yet or done her make-up and he wished that she didn't have to. That she could just stay as she was, with her hair casually spilling over her shoulders. That they could stay on Whydah and make love and play croquet and go for a swim. Because she had kept her word. He could tread water now and move forward and back and soon he would be swimming.

Only none of it was real. At best, it was window dressing.

He was Ondine's husband in name only, and soon enough he would be named as the father on his child's birth certificate. So many signatures on so many pieces of paper.

Switching his gaze to the window, he stared across the expanse of blue to where a dark line edged with gold cut across the sky. *We'll work it out.* That was what he'd said to Ondine. But how to do that, and what 'worked out' would look like were as distant and unreachable in his mind as the horizon.

It wasn't like all those weeks ago when Ondine had told him she was pregnant. Back then he had been so focused on the statistical improbability of his being a parent that his mind had been impervious to any persuasion. Of course, the truth had been there all along. If he had paid a little more attention to what was right in front of his face, asked a few pertinent questions, he would have known that it wasn't just possible he was the father, but highly probable. But blinkered by the fear that he would be unable to undo the damage of the past or, worse, that he would recreate it, he had deliberately, determinedly done neither of those things.

Now, though, he knew he was the father. Knew it with the same, unshakeable certainty that he knew his name, almost as if he had always known, right from that moment in the gallery when she'd bolted for the restroom.

And it blew his mind that he had created a new life. Every time he thought about it, it felt like an earthquake inside him.

Because making a baby didn't mean you were qualified to raise it. Just look at his own mother and father. He felt his throat tighten so that it hurt to swallow. After the divorce they had been so eager to get rid of every reminder of one another that they had got rid of him too. They had edited him out of their lives so that now he was their son in name only.

But maybe, though, that would change today.

Thanks to the considerable gravitational pull of his grandfather's money, the Walcott Cup was the one day of the year when both his parents deigned to be in the same space as one another. Usually they were too wrapped up in their new lives to pay much attention to him. But this year would be different. For once, the spotlight would be on him, and for the right reasons. On the face of it, he had turned his life around. Finally, they would have to notice him. See the change.

His grandfather would see he was changed too. Utterly changed, and that was what he needed to focus on right now. That, after all, was what all of this was about. And this was his turf. He knew these people. He understood the rules. He knew how to leverage his looks and his charm and his status. He could make this work.

Making his way through the country club, he felt almost euphoric. He knew most of the guests by name, and those he didn't were unimportant. And he couldn't remember why he had wanted Ondine not to get dressed up.

As if she knew what he was thinking, she glanced up at him and he felt her blue gaze like a punch. She looked exquisite in a simple white dress that perfectly offset her sun-kissed limbs. Her hair was in some kind of low bun and she was wearing a fascinator in the shape of an over-sized flower. And he was enthralled. Watching her smile and talk, as though this were something she did every day, only deepened his fascination.

He had thought she would be out of her depth. But Ondine was as strong a swimmer on land as she was in the water. She was making it look easy, he thought as she turned towards him again, her eyes catching fire as they met his. He felt her gaze burn through him, the lick of heat making his stomach drop so that it was the most natural thing in the world to pull her against him and kiss her hungrily.

'Everything okay?' he murmured.

She nodded. 'Everything's fine.'

His hand touched the nape of her neck, and then his eyes snagged on a woman's profile in the crowd. Tilted up to the sunlight, her eyes resting adoringly on the tall young man by her side, and suddenly he couldn't seem to make his breath reach his lungs. He stood frozen in the middle of the shifting mass of people, waiting for her to notice him, but after a moment she said something to an older man standing beside her and they all turned and moved as one towards the clubhouse.

And with every step they took, he could feel himself losing shape. As if he weren't part of the world, as if nobody could see him.

He felt a rush of panic, and then Ondine's hand found his, and that was better. He tightened his grip so that the ring on her finger pinched his skin, and some of the numbness in his chest retreated, and he felt present and connected again. But he needed to move and, looking down at Ondine, he said, 'We should go find my grandfather.'

It turned out that the Palm Beach Polo Club was actually an exclusive members-only country club. But then titles could be misleading, Ondine thought as Jack led her through the chattering groups of immaculately dressed men and long-limbed women.

Look at her: she was Mrs Jack Walcott. But her marriage was a sham, a pretence designed to reinstate her husband in his grandfather's good books.

And she had known that right from the start. Only somehow she had forgotten that their marriage wasn't real.

It wasn't only the sex. Or the baby. Or the way he had been there for her when she was throwing up and half crazy with hormones. Or even how he had comforted her, twice now. Holding her close and pushing the past back where it belonged. Because he had done that; he was the reason why she wasn't angry with Garrett and Vince any more. She just hadn't realised that yesterday.

At the centre of it all was Jack. He had changed her. Awoken her. Freed her. He had led her out of the dark, baffling woods back onto the path.

She glanced up at his handsome face.

But only so that she could meet John D. Walcott IV. He was the reason she was here. But yesterday, in the moment when Jack realised that he was the father of their baby, she had lost sight of that. She had fallen into the silence between her heartbeats.

She thought back to how he had held her close, close enough that she could feel the tension in his body as if he might break into a thousand pieces.

Somehow they had made it up to the bedroom and even as he'd been pulling her close she had been sliding her hands over his beautiful, strong body, some deep-buried instinct telling her that she must hold onto him. That if she just kept holding onto him, then they could make it work as he'd said.

She wanted to believe him, but the next day, he'd got up while she was sleeping. Today he'd let her lie in, so that there had been no time to talk before they'd had to leave. And now, they were back in Florida.

Gazing down at the pristine rectangle of grass, Ondine felt a sharp pang, almost like homesickness for the croquet lawn at Red Knots. After the tranquillity of Whydah Island, the country club felt more like a nightclub. It was so noisy and there were so many people milling around her.

Actually, it was Jack they were milling around. He was at their centre too. A glittering, dazzling sun. All laughter and light. The most heavenly of bodies around which smaller, duller planets orbited. And it wasn't hard to see why. Her breath caught in her throat. He looked gorgeous in a pale blue linen suit and tan loafers.

Jack, though, seemed oblivious. 'We should go find my grandfather.' His gaze shifted to a point past her shoulder, eyes narrowing, body straining forward in that unmistakable way of someone seeing the person they were looking for in a crowd. She felt his hand tighten around hers, she tensed for the moment of reckoning when she would finally meet John D. Walcott IV, but then he turned abruptly and began towing her in the opposite direction.

'He'll probably be down by the pony lines.'

'Pony lines?'

As he turned to look at her, she felt her stomach flip. It was almost as though he didn't recognise her. But he was the one who had changed, she thought, her stomach somersaulting now as she glanced up at his high, hard cheekbones and softly curving mouth. Not outwardly. And not to anyone who didn't know him. But she was so attuned to his every move, to each and every breath he took, and there was a tautness to him as if he was holding himself in check. The relaxed, care-free man of the last few days had vanished, and with shock she realised that he was acting again.

'It's where the ponies wait. He likes to go and see them before the match. I think it reminds him of when he used to play. Although he only stopped playing a year ago.'

'But he's in his eighties!'

'And very stubborn. He only stopped because he has osteoarthritis in his shoulder. He still rides, though.'

Watching his face soften, she felt her heart slip sideways. It was one of the many things she didn't understand about Jack Walcott. That he could lie to a man he so clearly adored. Then again, up until today he'd only had to manage that contradiction over the phone. Now he was going to have to lie to his grandfather in person. They both were.

Only right now, she couldn't think about her part in those lies. This was about Jack. She had to stay focused for him. Her stomach cartwheeled. And for Oli. This was about him too, his future, and it shocked her to think that she had forgotten that momentarily. No, not forgotten, she corrected herself. It was just that at some point between signing the marriage certificate and flying down to Florida, it had stopped being Ondine and Jack conspiring for their own ends and become two people whose goals were inseparable and symbiotic.

'It'll be okay.' She squeezed his hand and, after a moment, his fingers tightened around hers. 'We can do this. Together. We can show him that you've changed.'

For a second, his eyes locked with hers, and then they narrowed past her shoulder only this time his face lit up and he started to smile. 'Grandpa.'

'Jack.'

Ondine turned, her heart thudding unevenly in her chest as John Walcott embraced his grandson, and then turned towards her, smiling. He held out both his hands. 'Ondine. It's a pleasure to meet you,' he said, kissing her on both cheeks.

If she'd wondered what Jack would look like in fifty years, now she knew. John Walcott had the same jawline and the same patrician nose. Only his eyes were different, and of course his hair was grey, but he was still a handsome man.

'You look so like Jack,' she said, without thinking.

He laughed. 'Once upon a time, maybe. I'm so pleased you are here, my dear. Welcome to our family and—' his brown eyes dropped to the slight swell of her stomach '—congratulations.'

'Thank you.'

'I couldn't be more happy for you both.'

He turned towards his grandson. 'Let's walk back up to the box, and you can tell me everything you've been up to.'

John Walcott didn't just look like Jack, he was every bit as charming, and it was clear that he doted on his grandson. And in his presence, Jack seemed to shed that strange tension of earlier.

'Now tell me, Ondine, have you ever watched a polo match before?' John Walcott said as they took their seats.

She shook her head. 'No, but, from what Jack told me, it sounds a lot like croquet on horseback but with goals instead of wickets.'

He laughed again. 'That's not a bad analogy—'

'Jack said you used to play.' Glancing over to where the sleek, muscular players and their equally sleek, muscular ponies were warming up on the pitch, that fact seemed even more astonishing.

'I did. And if it wasn't for my grandson here, fussing over me, I would probably still be playing.' Reaching out, he squeezed Jack's shoulder. 'But he's right, I'm not as young as I was. Not as young as I'd like to be. Fortunately, I have Jack to look out for me.'

He smiled and Ondine smiled back, but it seemed odd that Jack should be that person. Didn't his son look out for him?

Jack was shaking his head. 'By looking out, he means I hid his mallets.'

'And I appreciate it. That's why I'd like you to present the cup for me this year.'

'I'm not going to do that, Grandpa, it's your tournament—'

'No, it's the Walcott Cup, and you are a Walcott, and it's time I took a step back. And it could be your first public job as chair of the foundation.'

Something passed across Jack's face. 'You think I'm ready for that?'

His grandfather nodded. 'I do. And other things too, perhaps.'

Watching the two Walcott men smile at one another, Ondine didn't know how to feel. A part of her was happy. It was what Jack wanted. And she wanted it too, but if his grandfather reinstated him then where did that leave her? The answer to that question made her wish that she could just take a time-out like the players and ponies, go somewhere where she wasn't on display. Where she didn't have to smile on demand. Because she didn't feel like smiling any more.

'So when's Dad getting here?' Jack said, leaning forward, his eyes scanning the crowds of spectators who were making their way into the stands.

His grandfather's smile was suddenly a little forced. 'He won't be joining us, I'm afraid. Something came up. I'm sure he'll call you later and explain.'

There was not a flicker of reaction on Jack's perfect face, or even in his golden eyes, but he went still. Even his smile seemed to freeze. 'Why can't he come?'

'Apparently, Annie brought her boyfriend home for the weekend. She's always been so secretive. I think they felt they needed to show support.'

'Of course they did.' His words were carefully neutral, but she felt the muscles of his arm tense against her, only then his grandfather was leaning forward in his chair and she saw the umpire in his black-and-white-striped shirt toss the ball into the melee of ponies and players.

CHAPTER TEN

THE POLO WAS EXCITING. But Ondine found it difficult to concentrate. The whole time she was distracted by the change in Jack's mood. Obviously he was disappointed his father had changed his plans, but was it that big a deal? Surely they could meet him on another day.

After the first match, there was an interlude when all the spectators walked onto the pitch and trod the 'divots'. Around them people were consciously not looking over in that way they did when you knew they wanted to just stop and stare, and it was a relief to return to the relative privacy of the box.

'Excuse me, Mr Walcott.' A steward wearing one of the club's branded royal-blue polo shirts stepped forward, blushing as both Jack and his grandfather nodded. 'I meant you, Mr Walcott,' she said, smiling at the older man. 'Mr Wood wondered if he could have a word.'

'Of course. Would you excuse me, Ondine? I'll be right back.'

Jack watched his grandfather make his way towards the clubhouse. 'Come on.' Grabbing her hand, he pulled her to her feet. 'Let's go.'

'Where are we going?' She was having to run

almost to keep up with his purposeful strides.
'Jack, can you slow down—?'

'Sorry,' he said automatically. He turned, his
face taut and unreachable as it had been in the
bathroom all those weeks ago. 'I just want to get
out of here before my grandfather comes back.'

'What?' She frowned up at him in shock. 'We
can't leave.'

'We can. And we are.' He started to pull her
forward, but she jerked her hand free.

'We can't just leave, Jack. You're going to present the cup, remember?'

'No, I'm not. Look, I'll just tell Grandpa that
you were feeling sick.' His eyes were unreadable
behind his sunglasses but the tendons in his jaw
were pulled tight. 'He won't mind.'

'But I do. I'm not lying to your grandfather.'

'Seriously? You want to take the moral high
ground on this one?' His lip curled dismissively.
'I think it's a bit late to worry about that.'

Her stomach twisted in shock, and she clutched
at the front of her dress to steady herself. The
truth hurt. What hurt more was Jack throwing it
in her face. But what hurt the most was the ache
in his voice.

It wrenched at something inside her so that instead of turning and walking away, she stepped
forward and pulled off his sunglasses. 'Yes, it is.
And it's hypocritical too, and I'm going to have

to find a way to live with that. But we came here today to show your grandfather that you're a different man from the one he sent away and if we leave now, then it's going to make it look as if nothing's changed.'

She saw a flicker of pain in his eyes, and a kind of angry bewilderment 'Nothing has.'

'That's not true.' Her eyes locked with his. 'I see you, Jack. I know who you are and you're not the same man I pulled out of the water. But you have to believe that. Otherwise no one else will.'

'I don't know if I can do this—' He was shaking his head; his voice sounded strained. 'I thought it would be different, I thought they'd be different—'

They? She stared at him in confusion, but there was no time to ask what he meant. His grandfather would be returning to the empty box at any moment.

'Maybe you can't. But *we* can.' She found his hand. 'Where you go, I go, so if you want to leave I'll come with you, but I think we should stay and finish this. And then we can go home.'

He was staring at her as if he was trying to read her face, see beneath the surface.

'Okay,' he said finally. 'We'll stay.'

The second match was equally thrilling but Ondine got the feeling that Jack wasn't even watching. That his eyes weren't tracking the spirited ponies as they dashed up and down the pitch, but scanning the crowd. But at least he was there, she thought, as the captain of the winning team stepped forward to receive their prize.

'Here. I want you to do it.' Ondine blinked. Jack was holding out the shining trophy. 'That's okay, isn't it, Grandpa?'

'It's better than okay, it's perfect.'

As the team celebrated their victory, John Walcott took hold of Ondine's hands and squeezed them. He was smiling but his eyes were bright with tears. 'My wife always used to present the trophy. She would be so pleased, so thank you—'

'No, thank you for inviting me today. But would it be all right if Jack took me home?' She glanced over to where he was shaking hands with the losing team. 'I just suddenly feel so tired.'

'Of course...of course.'

'I don't suppose I could email you something, could I?' She hesitated. 'It's something Jack's been working on. I know he wants you to read it, but—'

'I'll take a look. I promise.'

After the noise and heat of the day, the plane's interior was blissfully quiet and cool.

They were in the bedroom. Ondine gazed over to where Jack sat staring out of the window. She had told his grandfather that she was tired but it was Jack who looked shattered.

He hadn't spoken in the car on the way back to the airfield but he had kept hold of her hand. Now, though, he seemed remote, and it reminded her of her fake honeymoon at Red Knots when they had sat at opposite sides of the room. Then she had been too furious to speak. Now she didn't know what to say. Except the truth.

'Your grandfather is a lovely man,' she said quietly.

He nodded. 'He liked you.'

'I liked him. I'm sorry your parents couldn't make it, but we could arrange another date.'

A muscle flickered in his jaw. 'That won't be necessary.'

Not necessary.

She stared at him, wondering if she had misheard. 'Of course, it's necessary. They're your mum and dad. I can't not meet them. Your grandfather said that your dad was going to call you so just sort something out then.'

He was shaking his head. 'He's not going to call—'

'Then call him. And then call your mum.'

'That's not going to happen.'

'Because they didn't come to the polo.' She'd forgotten this, hadn't she? This version of Jack. The handsome, spoiled brat used to getting his own way. 'You're acting like a child. Things happen—'

'Things happen?' he echoed. 'You don't know what you're talking about. You don't know anything about what happens and you certainly don't know anything about me.'

'I know you're angry.' Blood was thudding in her ears. 'And I know you were going to leave the tournament without saying goodbye to your grandfather even though he asked you to present the trophy. I know that you wanted to use me to lie to him—'

She broke off, out of breath.

'I shouldn't have done that.' Jack's voice was faint or maybe it was just that she couldn't hear it above the pounding of her heart. 'I just needed a reason—'

There was a silence.

'You were wrong. My mother did come to the polo.' His mouth twisted. 'She was there. I saw her.'

She was there? Her eyes fluttered to his face.

'You don't believe me, do you?' he said into the silence. 'But I saw her just before we went to find my grandfather.'

Her breath scratched at her throat. 'But why didn't she come over?'

He shrugged. 'You need to ask her.'

I thought they'd be different.

Jack's words echoed inside her head. She'd wondered who he meant by 'they'. Now, though, she had a glimmer of understanding, but only Jack could confirm her suspicion. She looked at him, at his still, tense body.

'Or you could tell me.'

The seconds ticked by. 'I don't really have much of a relationship with my parents,' he said finally. 'They got divorced when I was four, and then they both remarried pretty quickly and had more children. I guess I was in the way.'

In the way.

Ondine stared at him in shock. How could he be in the way? He was their son.

As if he could read her thoughts, Jack smiled crookedly. 'I wasn't an easy child. I had a lot of tantrums, and I had night terrors too. My parents found it easier to outsource me to a nanny.'

His expression was bleak. 'Actually, I had two nannies, one for each house, only that gave my parents something else to argue about, and the nannies got caught in the crossfire so they were always leaving. I think I averaged about five a year. But then everything changed.'

'What happened?'

For a moment, he didn't reply, and she held her breath as the silence stretched and stretched. And then he said slowly, 'I suppose if you were being charitable you'd call it a screw-up.'

He pressed his fingers into his forehead as if he were drawing out a memory. 'I was at my dad's and my mum was flying back from St Barts to pick me up, only then I found out he was taking my sisters—half-sisters—to the beach house and I had a tantrum because I wanted to go too.'

The skin was pulled taut over his cheekbones.

'Obviously that wasn't an option so, to distract me, my dad told me we could play hide-and-seek. And I went off to hide. I had this really good place in the airing cupboard, and I waited and I waited and then I heard a door slam and I knew my mum must have arrived. But I wanted my dad to find me so I stayed hidden, only I must have fallen asleep because I woke up and the house was dark.'

She felt herself tense. 'Why was it dark?'

'Because everyone had left.'

He spoke in a matter-of-fact way but she felt her face dissolve with shock. Her heart was racing. 'I don't understand,' she said slowly. Because she didn't. Before their deaths, she and Oli were at the centre of her parents' world. And Jack's family was wealthy, educated. They had child-care on tap. It made her mind boggle to think his father could leave his child home alone. Yes, in a film it would be funny, but she didn't feel like laughing. She felt sick now, sicker than she had in those first tumultuous months of her pregnancy.

'Nobody meant for it to happen. I think my dad was worried that if he came and found me I'd have another tantrum when he had to leave, so it was easier for him to just go. To be fair, Holly, the housekeeper, was there. Only she was in the garden when he drove away, and she must have thought I'd gone with him, so she locked up the house and left.'

'What about your mother?'

'She'd decided to extend her holiday so she was still in St Barts.'

Anger knifed through her. 'Without telling your dad?'

'She did tell him. She left a message. But they were always leaving messages and I guess he just didn't bother picking it up. Like I said. It was a screw-up.'

'But they must have realised and come back—'

'Nobody came back.'

His eyes were tired, empty, lost, and, sliding off the bed, she knelt in front of him and took hold of his hands. 'You must have been so scared.'

'I was a kid. I didn't really understand what had happened at first but then I realised I was locked in the house on my own and then I panicked. I got up onto a chair to try and slide one of the bolts on the back door. Only I fell off and broke my arm.'

Her lungs felt as if they might burst. Each word he spoke hurt more than the last.

'I didn't know at the time, but I triggered the alarm system and the security company saw me on the camera feed and called my grandfather and he came and took me to the hospital. I don't know what he said to my parents but after that I went to live with him.'

Jack looked down at his hands, and she saw that they were shaking. 'He's the only person who's ever looked out for me. And I lied to his face.'

Now she took his hands and held them tight. 'Not about what matters. Your grandfather wanted you to take stock of your life, and you have. And I saw how much he loves you, and he's always going to love you. He just wants you to love yourself.'

'I've hurt him. I do stupid things. Reckless things.'

'Like on the yacht,' she said quietly.

He nodded. 'I didn't lie to you. I wasn't drunk or high. And I didn't want to be there any more but I jumped because I saw this photo of my mum and Penn at some tennis match, and I got upset—'

There was a long pause. Outside the window, the sky was growing darker.

'I don't know why it happens but I start to feel numb—'

His hands tightened around hers. 'It's like I'm disappearing into this darkness and I need someone to come find me or I'll disappear for ever, and the only way I can stop it is by doing something that hurts or scares me. Because then I can focus on that and it brings me back, and I know that's not okay—'

'Oh, Jack—' Clasping his face, she kissed him gently. 'No, it's not okay.' She felt suddenly and intensely protective of him. 'But it will be.'

He buried his face into her hair. 'I'm sorry about what I said earlier. And how I was before about the baby. I know I'm the father, and I want to be there for you, for both of you. And I don't know how we can make it work or even if you want to try—'

'I do—' She bit her lip to stop herself from crying. 'I do want that; I want you to be part of this.' She took his hand and laid it gently against her stomach.

'You do?' He seemed stunned. And it hurt that he should feel that way. That he had been hurt so often, so badly. But it was never going to happen again, she thought fiercely. She wasn't going to let it happen. And it was in that moment as she squared up to the world that it hit her.

She loved him. And just thinking it made her heart blossom like a flower.

Pressing her forehead against his, she closed

her eyes, accepting the truth. Duty had sent her thundering into the water, but love was the reason she had taught him to swim. And why she had forced him to stay at the polo. She wanted what was best for him. She wanted him to be happy.

Only Jack wasn't talking about love. He was talking about making things work, and if her two previous marriages had taught her anything, it was that love had to be mutual.

She took a breath. 'We can make this work. We will make it work.'

He slid down beside her and they held each other close for a long time. At first, it wasn't about sex. It was about knowing that they had each other. But then she pressed a kiss to his mouth, and he was kissing her back. They didn't take off their clothes or get onto the bed. He pulled up her skirt and lifted her onto his lap and pushed into her.

Afterwards, she rested her head against his shoulder, feeling his shuddering heart until, finally, he loosened his arms. Tipping her off his lap, he got to his feet. 'I'm going to go speak to the pilot.' Leaning forward, he kissed her softly on the mouth. 'I need to give them enough time to change course.'

'Change course?' She frowned. 'Aren't we going back to the island?'

'Whydah wasn't for real. It was just a honeymoon.' His dark gold eyes fixed on her face. 'This is real life now.'

'So where are we going?'

'To New York.' He reached down and pulled her to her feet. Now his hands cupped her belly. 'We're going home.'

Flicking on the TV, Jack stared at the screen dazedly, watching the news ticker slide across the bottom. He felt as if he had woken from a deep sleep to find that, incredibly, the world had kept spinning and people were going on with their lives. But up here in his apartment, that all felt like a charade. And yes, the irony of that was not lost on him.

He had left Ondine in the pool to come downstairs and make breakfast. Not personally. He wasn't sure he'd ever switched on the stove before. But he was an expert at ordering breakfast. And maybe he could learn to cook. It was not something he'd considered doing before but that was the difference between the old Jack and the new. Things that had previously been off-limits felt possible, achievable. Like learning to swim. Or being a father. Ondine had made him realise that he had choices. That he wasn't condemned to staying the same.

Two days had passed since they had landed in New York. They had spent almost the entire time in bed, neither of them quite ready to leave the honeymoon behind. But then, they'd realised that they didn't have to. That it wasn't an either/or situation.

His fingers bit into the kitchen counter. Given a choice, both his parents would have opted for the other to keep him. And arriving in New York, he'd wondered why he had been so compelled to admit that to Ondine. He'd never told anyone about his childhood before. He'd felt too ashamed and scared that once they knew the real Jack Walcott they too would turn away like his parents. That they would see that he wasn't worth loving. Worth keeping.

But Ondine hadn't turned away, he thought, remembering that blaze of outrage in her eyes. She hadn't sided with his parents. She had stayed and listened and held him and then she'd told him she wanted him in her life and the baby's.

His heart beat lightly inside his chest. The baby. His baby. Their child. Ondine had been right. It was a miracle. Not just her getting pregnant against all the odds, but this new-found belief that he could be a father. A hands-on dad.

And believing that to be possible had rubbed away the last of the jagged edges. There were still bad memories, but they felt distant and softer now, as if he were looking at them through water. And he felt calmer, even when he was on his own, and that was the litmus test. Usually, he couldn't bear to be by himself, but right now, he was enjoying the quiet of the apartment. It meant he could hear the distant back and forth of the traffic; it reminded him of the sea around Whydah.

And Whydah made him think about Ondine. But that was hardly surprising. She was in his thoughts all the time.

When he could actually hold a thought.

His breath caught in his throat, his body tightening as he remembered the soft, choking noises she'd made as she'd shuddered against his mouth earlier. He wanted her all the time. Wanted her so badly it made his bones ache. But it wasn't just the sex. They had talked about her life with Oli, about her parents and her childhood. And he had told her about where he liked to buy bagels. And about walking the High Line. And the bar where they made their own spiced nuts. Nothing was off-limits. They shared everything.

Jack frowned. Something was buzzing. Not his phone. He glanced at the oven warily, and then he spotted Ondine's phone at the other end of the counter.

Glancing at the name on the screen, he felt a jolt of anticipation.

It was Oliver. For a moment, he hesitated. They hadn't been formally introduced yet, but he knew that she wanted him to like her brother and it would make her happy to come down and find the two of them getting on.

He tapped the screen. There was a slight lag, and he wondered momentarily what time it was in Costa Rica, and then Oliver's face appeared, young, grinning, relaxed, excited—

'Hi, On—' His smile froze, then faded a fraction as he saw Jack.

'Oh, I'm sorry, I thought you were—'

'Ondine.' Jack smiled. 'She's at the pool but she should be down any minute.'

He watched in amusement as Oliver slapped his forehead with the flat of his hand. 'I thought I'd catch her before she went to work.' His face stiffened. 'You're not her boss, are you?'

It took Jack longer than it should have to make sense of what Oliver was asking. But he didn't understand what he had heard. Or perhaps he had misheard it. It was the only explanation, because Oliver must know that Ondine had left Whitecaps months ago. And why hadn't he recognised him? Even without the name on screen, he would know instantly who Oli was.

'No, I'm not her boss,' he managed to say.

Even from eight thousand miles away, Oli's relief was palpable. 'Okay, I know she can't really talk at work so I'll give her a call back later. Sorry, I'm Oliver, by the way, her brother…' The silence stretched between them as Oliver politely waited for him to provide his name.

'I'm Jack.'

Oliver smiled. 'Nice to meet you, Jack.' Still smiling, he hung up.

Jack stared down at the phone in his hand, his heart pounding. He couldn't seem to move. There had been no flicker of recognition when he'd told Oli his name. But that didn't make any sense. If it did that could mean only one thing. Ondine hadn't told her brother she was married.

Only that couldn't be true. Why wouldn't she have told him? Oli was her only family. Surely she would want him to know something that significant. Surely she would have to let him know if she meant what she said on the plane about making things work.

His heart shivered inside his chest. Unless, of course, she hadn't meant it. She had simply said what was expedient in the moment to placate him. Like his father offering to play hide-and-seek.

He was still standing at the counter, frozen as if made of ice, when Ondine came into the kitchen.

Her hair was still damp from the pool and she was wearing one of his T-shirts over bare legs. The bump of her stomach pressed against the fabric. She had never looked more beautiful or natural. But looks could be deceptive.

As she slid her arms around his body his throat tightened, his body too, and it would be so easy to pull that T-shirt over her head and lift her onto the counter and lose himself in the slick heat between her thighs.

But instead he stepped backwards, his hands on hers, peeling her arms away from his waist.

'What is it?' She looked up at him, her blue eyes widening. 'Are you okay?'

She sounded worried; looked worried too, and he wanted to believe what he was hearing and seeing but—

He tapped her phone. 'Oli called.'

Her face softened as it always did when her brother was mentioned. 'That's okay. I can speak to him later.'

I can speak to him later.

Her words rolled around inside his head, like bottles on a bar-room floor. Had he ever seen her speak to Oli in real time? The answer to that question made him reach out and steady himself against the counter.

'You don't need to,' he said slowly. 'I spoke to him.'

And it was then, still watching her face, that any hopes he had that he was wrong were lost. Shattered. Relinquished.

There was silence. Now she was unnaturally still.

'He doesn't know about us. About the marriage.' He phrased it as a statement. Because he could tell from the shock on her face that he didn't need to ask the question. And then a new realisation rose like nausea in his throat. 'He doesn't know about the baby.'

'I was going to tell him.' Her voice was faint and scratchy as if the words were rough-edged. She reached out, and he flinched as she touched his arm.

'I just wanted to find the right time. When things were settled.'

He stared at her disbelieving, angry, hurting in a way that made him long for the numbness of before. 'Why bother? Why not just deny everything?'

She blinked as he threw her words back in her face.

'That's not what I was doing—'

'Oh, please—' He spun away from her into the living room, needing distance from her, from the shock and pain of her betrayal.

'It's exactly what you're doing. You know how I know that? Because I was doing it back on Whydah.'

His hands clenched and, glancing down, he stared at them dazedly as if they belonged to someone else.

'That was different. You hadn't accepted the baby was yours—'

His eyes dropped to her stomach. 'And what? You're punishing me for that?'

She took a step towards him. 'No, of course not. It's not even about you. It's about Oli. I didn't know what to say to him.' Her voice stumbled but he could see the fierce love in her eyes for her brother. 'He doesn't have anyone else but me, and he needs me. And I know he's super-smart, but you spoke to him. He's just a kid.'

'And I spoke to you. I told you things I've never told anyone. Because I trusted you—'

'You can trust me—' she began, but he was backing away from her.

'You told me that we could make this work. That we would make it work.' He was shivering now so that he had to tense his body to keep his voice from shaking. 'But you know what, Ondine? I'm really struggling to see how you could believe that when you haven't even told your brother I exist.'

Suddenly, he couldn't bear to be in the room with her any longer, to have her witness his stupidity. Without giving her a chance to reply, he turned and walked across the living room and into the hall and slammed his hand against the elevator button. The doors opened immediately, and he stepped inside, his heart pounding.

'Jack—'

He caught a glimpse of her pale, stunned face and then the doors shut and a moment later the elevator started to move. He didn't know where he was going. But it didn't matter anyway. What mattered was to keep moving. Because if he stopped, he knew the pain in his heart would swallow him whole.

CHAPTER ELEVEN

As the doors closed Ondine felt as if she were back on Dipper's Beach. Only the difference was she couldn't dive after him into the elevator shaft. Instead, she hammered the button on the wall with her fist, again and again, but she knew already the lift would only come back up when Jack stepped through the doors in the entrance foyer. It was one of the perks of having the penthouse: you had your own private elevator.

But it didn't feel like a perk now. Panic clawed at her throat, strangling her.

Where was he going? Above her frantic heartbeat she could hear his voice inside her head.

'I got upset... I don't know why it happens but I start to feel numb...and the only way I can stop it is by doing something that hurts or scares me.'

And now she was scared. Pressing her hand to her mouth, she gave a sob as the lift doors opened. It was empty. He was gone because of her. She had hurt him. She hadn't meant to, but she had. Somewhere out there in Manhattan he was hurting—

Head spinning, she stared at the empty lift, panic and fear overwhelming her. She had known instantly what to do on the beach even though she'd been off duty and had no float, no phone—

Her phone.

Her heart stopped beating. Of course. She could call him.

She ran back into the apartment and snatched up her phone. Her fingers felt fat and clumsy as she pressed his name on the screen.

'Pick up, pick up…please pick up,' she whispered. She felt a jolt of relief as he answered and then she realised it was just his voicemail greeting.

'Hi, this is Jack. Leave a message and I'll get back to you.'

'It's me. I'm so sorry, Jack. I know I hurt you and I know you probably don't want to speak to me right now, but could you please call me back?'

She texted him too, and then she sat down on the sofa. She had to. Her legs felt as if they were made of blancmange. Even after her parents died, she hadn't felt this helpless. Then there had been so much to arrange, to organise, and she'd had to be strong for Oli. But here in this beautiful, silent apartment with his accusations still ringing in the air, she couldn't catch her breath, let alone think of what to do next.

The room swam. She had never meant to hurt him. She loved him, and now she realised how much because pain was the price you paid for loving someone. She knew that from losing her parents and this pain was equal to the aching loss she'd felt after the accident.

Think. *Think.* There must be something she could do. She couldn't just sit here and do nothing. But this was her first time in New York. Aside from Jack, she knew no one. Knew nothing about the city.

Except that wasn't true. They had talked a lot about his life here, she thought, her heartbeat accelerating. She knew where he bought coffee. And where he liked to walk. And he had a driver, Tom, who had picked them up from the airport.

She felt a fluttering hope, tiny but strong like a hummingbird's wings. Surely with Tom's help she would be able to find him, and then she could talk to him. She could make this right. But first she needed to get dressed. And call him again.

An hour and a half later, that hope was growing feebler by the minute. Nobody had seen Jack at any of the places she went to. And New York was so much bigger than she had imagined. A man could get lost there with hardly any effort. If he was even there.

Maybe he had left the city. She pictured the Walcott jet gleaming on the runway, her heart a leaden beat of misery. Left the country.

If only she had told Oli the truth. But when could she have told him? And what? At the beginning she had been struggling to believe that she could go through with it. That she would marry Jack for money. After the ceremony she had been angry with herself, mainly for having left herself so few options. Too angry to speak to Oli. He would have heard it in her voice. She couldn't have risked that. Couldn't have risked him coming back.

Then later she had been sick and then there was the baby and how could she have told him about the baby?

'Is there anywhere else you'd like to go, Mrs Walcott?'

Her pulse quickened. There was one place left they hadn't tried. 'Could we go back to the apartment, please, Tom?' she said quickly.

And then she offered up a prayer. *Please let him be there. Let him be safe.*

As the elevator doors opened she ran back into the apartment.

'Jack? Jack—' She called his name as she checked each room in turn. But the apartment was as still and silent as before.

She sat down on the sofa, her phone trembling in her hand. She had called him thirty times now, left as many messages, and it was obvious he didn't want to talk to her. Remembering how he had pulled away from her, she felt as if she were drowning. Her hand reached instinctively to protect her stomach, and she forced herself to breathe. What mattered was finding Jack, making him safe. Only she couldn't do that if he wouldn't talk to her.

Her heart leapt to her throat as her phone rang shrilly. 'Jack—'

There was a beat of silence. 'Ondine, it's John Walcott. I'm back in New York, and I was just calling to invite you both to lunch on Sunday.' Another beat of silence. 'Is everything all right, my dear?'

She pressed her hand against her mouth. 'I don't think it is—'

'What's happened?' he said calmly. 'Is Jack not there?'

His simple question was what made her finally unravel.

'He left. And it's my fault. I let him down. I made him think I don't love him and I do. So much. Only he thinks I don't care—'

Jack had finally stopped shivering but he was still walking. He hadn't followed a particular route. In fact, half the time, he'd had no idea where he was. It was as if his limbs were acting of their own accord. His fingers too, he thought dully. He couldn't stop checking his phone, even though he knew that he shouldn't.

He couldn't bear to hear or read any more excuses. There had been so many over the years. So many betrayals to forgive and forget dating back to before he was too young to even understand the concept of either of those things. And it would break his heart to hear Ondine's voice repeat those same meaningless phrases, let alone have to read them in black and white.

Only why would his heart be affected? Ondine had clearly never seen their marriage as anything other than transactional.

His pulse stumbled, and, remembering the feel of her small, soft body in his arms as she told him about the misery of her first marriage, he felt his legs slow, then stop. People surged round him on the pavement, tutting and rolling their eyes, but he barely registered their irritation. He was too distracted by another memory, this time his grandfather talking about his grandmother.

'I suppose you could say I shared my soul. And that's when I realised I loved her. You see, that's what love is, Jack, sharing your soul.'

He had shared his soul with Ondine. More than that, he had opened his heart to her and the baby growing inside her. To a future he had never imagined for himself. A future with a woman he loved and their baby. A baby that would swim like a fish.

His phone vibrated, and as he glanced at the

screen some of the pain in his chest softened at the edges.

It was his grandfather.

He hesitated. He didn't want to keep lying. But if he didn't answer, his grandfather would worry. Only what could he say? How was he supposed to explain the tangle of lies he had spun with Ondine? Particularly now they turned out to be true—

There was only one thing he could do. Swiping the screen up, he said quickly, 'Can I call you back, Grandpa? There's someone I need to talk to.'

'I know. Ondine called me. And you do need to talk to her.' His grandfather's voice was quiet but firm. 'But first I need to talk to you.'

Pacing back across the living room, Ondine stared at her phone, willing it to ring. It was nearly an hour since John Walcott had called, and he still hadn't rung back. She had no idea what that meant, but sitting down made her feel like a butterfly on the end of a pin. Maybe she would go back and wait outside the apartment building, see if anyone coming in had another idea of where Jack could be.

She snatched up her phone. Then if John called she could—

The elevator doors opened and she felt her legs

go weak with relief as Jack walked into the entrance hall. He looked pale and tired, but he was here and he was safe.

'You came back—'

There was a silence. He seemed almost stunned to see her and she wondered if he'd thought she had left. She felt suddenly close to tears as he nodded slowly. 'I was walking around and I realised that I hadn't said everything I wanted to say.'

She could hear the struggle to keep his voice even. He felt betrayed, and maybe he wouldn't listen or believe her if he did, but she had to try and explain.

'I have too,' she said, hardly able to speak past the lump in her throat. 'I'm so sorry that I hurt you. I didn't mean to. I should have told Oli about us getting married, but I just couldn't get my head round what we were doing. And then I found out I was pregnant and I was ill and I was scared that if I told him, he'd be worried and want to come back and he's had so much to deal with. I didn't want him to have to worry about me, as well.'

Silence filled the hallway.

Jack stared at her. A muscle worked along his jaw. 'Is that it? Have you finished?'

She nodded, but he didn't speak, he just kept staring at her and then he said slowly, 'Nobody has ever looked out for me except my grandfather. I told you that on the plane, do you remember?'

He took a step forward. 'But I was wrong. You looked out for me too. Right from the start when you pulled me from the water. And then you stayed at the hospital and you watched me sleep. Even when I said awful things you didn't leave.'

'I did.' She thought back to Whydah. 'On the bluff, and after we played croquet.'

'And I deserved it both times. But you came back. Nobody's ever done that.'

'You deserve to be loved, Jack,' she whispered.

He took another step closer. 'And you went looking for me today. You made Tom take you around New York.'

'Did he tell you?'

He shook his head. 'My grandfather told me.' Leaning forward, he lifted a tendril of hair away from her face, tucking it behind her ear. 'Why did you go looking for me, O?'

She felt her heart melt. 'I couldn't not.'

Jack stared down into her eyes. 'What you said to my grandfather about loving me.' He was struggling to speak. 'Was that true? Because I love you.'

She covered her mouth with her hand, and he pulled her against him, wrapping his arms around her, holding her close against him so that she could feel his heart beating in time to hers.

'I love you,' he said again, and this time he smiled a smile that lit up his face and filled her with light and a happiness she had never known. 'You saved me, O. And I'm not talking about what happened in Palm Beach. I was drowning on dry land, and you saved me. You gave me the kiss of life. The kiss of love,' he said softly.

'You saved me too.' She felt his arms tighten around her and, looking up, she saw his golden eyes were glittering with tears. 'You make me feel special. You made me trust myself again.' She bit her lip. 'I thought I'd lost you—'

He breathed out shakily. 'You share my heart, my soul. You can't lose me. I belong to you.' His hand curved around her stomach. 'Both of you.'

Their mouths met blindly and they kissed just as they had that first day on the beach, and they were still kissing as he scooped her into his arms and carried her back into their apartment, their home.

EPILOGUE

THE GARDEN WAS starting to fill up. Guests were milling around the terrace, talking, laughing. Leaning forward to get a better view, Ondine watched as one of the animal handlers opened a brightly coloured carrier and two lop-eared rabbits hopped enthusiastically onto Red Knots' pristine lawn. 'It's getting pretty crowded down there,' she called over her shoulder.

'With people or animals?'

A flicker of heat danced over her skin as two warm hands slid round her waist, and Jack leaned in to drop a row of kisses down her throat.

'Both.'

'Who or what are we waiting for?'

His voice was casual but she knew what it cost him to ask that question. What it had cost for that question even to be possible. 'I think we're good to go,' she said softly, turning in his arms. 'Your dad is with your grandpa making friends with the ponies, and your mum is talking to Oliver.'

It was twenty months since she and Jack had stood in the Miami-Dade courthouse and exchanged vows. But the transactional relationship they had entered into that day bore no resemblance to their marriage now.

For starters, there were no more secrets. Everything was in the open. More importantly, the love they had promised one another was real. So real, she thought, looking up at him, her heart contracting so that it was suddenly difficult to breathe.

'You know we're never going to make it downstairs if you keep looking at me like that,' he said softly.

She reached out and touched his marvellous, miraculous face. 'Did I tell you how proud I am of you?'

His golden eyes were meltingly soft. 'I think you mentioned it a couple of times.'

She had. But she still liked to remind him. 'You made this happen.'

'The party!' He shook his head. 'That's all down to Martha's Farm Friends.'

'I'm not talking about the party. Well, I am. But I'm talking about why we can have a party with both our families. I'm talking about you reaching out—'

'And I could only do that because of you.' His hands firmed around the swell of her stomach. 'You're the best thing that ever happened to me, and I don't know where I would be now if I hadn't met you.'

'You'd be fine.' She touched his face lightly, letting him see her love and belief in him, and her gratitude for the life they made together. 'You're the best man I know. The best husband. The best dad, best CEO.'

His mouth curved slightly, acknowledging her words. He believed them. And there were no words for the way it made her feel to know that he did believe them. Getting to this point had been hard. He'd had to confront his past, his parents. And it was still a work in progress. But it was like swimming. You had to start with the basics and practise. Before you knew it, you were swimming triathlons for charity, she thought, her gaze snagging on the medals that were knotted casually around the bedpost. And she was proud of him for that too.

Jack looked down into Ondine's beautiful blue eyes, his heart beating in time to the distant waves. Most days he woke up and gave thanks to the ocean for bringing Ondine into his life. She had breathed, not just life into his lungs, but love into his heart. She had given him faith in himself. A beautiful daughter.

Speaking of whom…

'Do you think we should get the birthday girl up?' he said, stroking Ondine's hair. 'We wouldn't want her to miss her first party.' Their eyes met as, on cue, the baby monitor by the bed gave a squeak and then a satisfied kind of gurgle.

Esme Candace Walcott was standing up in her cot, her tousled blonde curls framing her face like a halo, a giraffe clutched in one chubby hand, the other reaching for Jack.

'Dada—'

Watching his daughter's wide blue eyes light up with delight and amazement, Jack felt his heart tumble in his chest. He gave thanks for his daughter too. If Ondine had cracked him open, Esme had pushed the crack apart and that was the thing when you opened up. You let the love in, and out. So much love.

He glanced at the row of soft toys lining one wall. Less room, though—

Tucking Esme against his shoulder, he turned to Ondine. 'You know, we should probably think about getting a bigger place when we get back to New York. Before this one arrives.' His hand reached out automatically to touch her stomach again. He couldn't stop himself. This was the part he'd missed out on before through fear and doubt. But he wasn't scared any more. And his doubts were normal, transitory, easily resolved.

'Or we could keep the apartment. Get some place upstate. With a bit of land. Kidnap some of Martha's animals.'

Ondine smiled. 'New Jack meet Old Jack.' And she loved both. Leaning into him, she wrapped her arm around his waist. 'I don't care where we live as long as we're together.'

They stood there for a moment, their bodies touching, both of them certain that wherever they lived, whatever was to come, it would all be just detail. What mattered was in their hearts and souls. There was no need for anything else.

* * * * *

If you were swept off your feet by
Her Diamond Deal with the CEO
then you'll fall in love with these other stories by Louise Fuller!

Beauty in the Billionaire's Bed
The Christmas She Married the Playboy
The Italian's Runaway Cinderella
Maid for the Greek's Ring
Their Dubai Marriage Makeover

Available now!